"Why did you drag me into doing this?"

"Because you're acting as my hostess, Kay. And it's a hostess's duty to greet her guests," York answered smoothly.

"They're not my guests. These are your wedding guests. I only agreed to act as hostess to your house party," Kay whispered furiously. "Goodness knows what all these people must be thinking, having me welcome them here tonight as if . . . as if . . ." Kay's voice faltered, her cheeks firing.

"As if what, Katie?" York mocked, daring her to finish her sentence and laughing as if he found the direction of her thoughts highly amusing.

Kay only glared back. Well, if he didn't care about her reputation or her feelings, here was one man who wasn't about to have his cake and eat it, too!

Sue Peters grew up in the idyllic countryside of
Warwickshire, England, and began writing romance
novels quite by chance. "Have a go," her mother
suggested when a national writing contest sponsored
by Mills and Boon appeared in the local newspaper.
Sue's entry placed second, and a career was born.
After completing her first romance novel, she missed
the characters so much she started another and
another.... Now she's as addicted to writing as she is
to gardening, which she often does as she's
formulating new plots.

Books by Sue Peters

HARLEQUIN ROMANCE

1975—CLOUDED WATERS
2030—ONE SPECIAL ROSE
2104—PORTRAIT OF PARADISE
2156—LURE OF THE FALCON
2204—ENTRANCE TO THE HARBOUR
2351—SHADOW OF AN EAGLE
2368—CLAWS OF A WILDCAT
2410—MARRIAGE IN HASTE
2423—TUG OF WAR
2471—DANGEROUS RAPTURE
2501—MAN OF TEAK
2583—LIGHTNING STRIKES TWICE
2812—NEVER TOUCH A TIGER

Don't miss any of our special offers. Write to us at the
following address for information on our newest releases.

Harlequin Reader Service
901 Fuhrmann Blvd., P.O. Box 1397, Buffalo, NY 14240
Canadian address: P.O. Box 603,
Fort Erie, Ont. L2A 5X3

Entrance to Eden

Sue Peters

Harlequin Books

TORONTO • NEW YORK • LONDON
AMSTERDAM • PARIS • SYDNEY • HAMBURG
STOCKHOLM • ATHENS • TOKYO • MILAN

Original hardcover edition published in 1987
by Mills & Boon Limited

ISBN 0-373-02892-X

Harlequin Romance first edition February 1988

Printed in U.S.A.

CHAPTER ONE

COURTNEY CATERERS. Receptions. Dinners. Private parties.

Kay gave the black and gold sign-writing on the side of the van an impulsive polish with her coat sleeve as she parked the smart little vehicle.

'Wait until Helen hears my news,' she anticipated gleefully, and hummed a light tune under her breath as she let herself into the cottage.

'I'm in the kitchen,' her sister's voice called out as Kay pushed the front door shut behind her.

'Coming.'

Kay padded along the hall towards the half-opened door at the end, from which came the tempting smell of fresh baking.

'Had a good day?' Helen looked up from her task of transferring a tray of dishes from the oven to the waiting worktop.

'Super! I managed to get the asparagus you wanted. It'll be delivered with the rest of the fruit and veg, first thing tomorrow morning.'

Kay hugged her secret to her until Helen should finish what she was doing, and strove to keep her voice matter of fact as she went on, 'I picked up a cricket bat and a set of stumps for Sam, too. It's just what he wanted. Is he still awake?'

'No.' Helen shook her head. 'He tried his hardest not to go to sleep. He's done a picture with that new box of paints you brought him, and he wanted to give it to you himself. But he was just too tired to last out until you got home, and I had to put him to bed. You spoil him,' she scolded Kay fondly, pausing in her task to examine the miniature bat and stumps Kay produced from her shopping bag. 'He's left the picture on the living-room table for you.'

'The doctors said his leg needed exercise, if he was ever

5

going to lose his limp,' Kay excused her generosity.

'I know.' Helen's eyes were shadowed as she bent again to the oven, and Kay left her, and went to collect the picture.

'It's always the same one, isn't it?' she remarked quietly, returning to the kitchen, and frowning down at the childish daub of brilliant blue background, liberally dotted with matchstick figures in various bright colours, easily identifiable as people swimming.

'Sam's notion of what a public swimming baths looks like?' His mother sighed, and adjusted the position of the dishes on the worktop with quite unnecessary care.

'If only he could get over his fear of travelling in a vehicle, I could take him to the swimming baths at Wychwood,' Kay regretted. 'We could go by bus, if he didn't want to travel in the van.'

'Swimming would be the best thing for his leg,' Helen agreed, 'but he won't travel, so that's that. Perhaps his new cricket set will help.'

'Let's hope so.' Kay changed the subject, striving to dispel the shadow. 'Who's that lot for?' She nodded towards the worktop. 'I didn't know we'd got any more orders for today.'

'Vanda Lane's throwing a supper party tonight.'

'She might have given us a bit more warning.'

'It was a last-minute arrangement. She phoned after you left this morning.'

'I suppose she left the choice of menu to you, as usual?' Kay asked drily, and strolled across to inspect the contents of the dishes on the worktop.

'Heavens,' she exclaimed, 'there's enough here to feed an army! Chilled consommé, smoked salmon curls, chicken and pineapple salad, and a cold quiche. I'm beginning to feel hungry myself, just looking at them.'

'There are peach meringues and fresh fruit kebabs, and a cheeseboard to follow. Vanda's providing the coffee and drinks herself.'

'She'll tire herself out,' Kay prophesied sarcastically. 'Vanda's got every imaginable gadget in her own kitchen, and she never lifts a finger to use any of them. If she cared to bestir herself, she could have done all this on her own, and saved herself the expense.'

'Be grateful she can't be bothered. It's the Vanda Lanes of this world who give us our living.'

'That's going to improve considerably from now on,' Kay gloated, unable to contain her secret any longer. 'I've landed a fabulous order today.'

'Put the kettle on while I finish setting the dishes on the worktop, then I can listen in peace,' Helen suggested and, seeing Kay's resigned look, added, 'You don't have to deliver the order. Vanda's husband is coming to collect it himself.'

'Now tell me,' she prompted, as the kettle whistled a warning, and Kay plumped down on to a kitchen stool and poured out the events of her day.

'I bumped into Louise Demster while I was in Wychwood this morning.'

'Isn't she the air hostess you used to talk about, while you were working with Oliver Tait? I thought she went abroad some time ago.'

'She's been on the Australian run for the past eighteen months, but she's back home again now. Not for long, though. She's getting married to an Australian pilot, and they're going out there to set up their own freight line.'

'Pity,' Helen grimaced. 'We could do with an extra wedding reception, to fill in the gaps in our order book.'

'That's just it,' Kay gloated. 'They're getting married over here, before they go. And Louise asked if we'd do her reception. It's short notice. The wedding's in six weeks' time.'

'We'll manage.' Helen brightened visibly. 'How many have we got to cater for?'

'Six hundred.' Kay dropped her bombshell.

'*Six hundred?* Kay, you know we can't! We haven't got the facilities to cater for so many. The biggest job we've taken on so far was for two hundred, and that stretched our capacity to the limit. What on earth possessed you to take on such an order?'

Helen's cup dropped with a clatter into her saucer, and she stared at her younger sister in total dismay.

'Calm down. It isn't as bad as it sounds. Really, it's three hundred twice. Three hundred guests for the wedding reception in the morning, and the same again for a buffet supper at the ball in the evening.'

'Even so, three hundred twice . . .' Helen demurred.

'We'll cope somehow. We *must*. Think what an advertisement it'll be for our business. It's just what we need to put us into the league for the big-time work,' Kay urged. 'Louise must have a wide circle of friends to invite such a crowd, and if we can make a good impression with the reception we provide, there's no knowing what it might lead to.'

Seated opposite to one another on the drop-on kitchen stools, the two sisters were remarkably alike, except that Helen, at thirty-seven, was eleven years Kay's senior, and the gold glints that lit the brown head of the younger girl were replaced by premature grey streaks in Helen's hair.

The latter looked frowningly round the spotless kitchen, assessing its capacity to cater for three hundred twice. The workroom was fitted out with the very latest in stainless steel and marble, the big double ovens still exuding a grateful warmth to combat the chill of the early spring evening.

Kay's glance followed that of her sister. The up-to-the-minute kitchen was their pride and joy. When they had bought the cottage between them, the expensive modern equipment they had installed in the adjoining bakery had eaten up the last of their slender resources, but they had made no compromise to economy, and deliberately aimed high, buying the best available on the market. During the intervening months their foresight had paid off handsomely in ease of working.

But six hundred meals in one day? Helen's doubts began to communicate themselves to Kay.

'It's an awful lot to cope with. I don't think we can, unless . . .' Helen paused, and then went on more hopefully, 'unless the reception's in the form of a cold buffet, and we can make the food beforehand, and freeze it.'

'That would fit in with the arrangements. They're hiring

a marquee for the reception. It's to be held at her brother's house.'

'She's taking a chance on the weather, having a marquee.'

'From what I can gather, Louise doesn't have any choice in the matter,' Kay retorted. 'She won't have a settled home in Australia until they've worked up the freight business, and decided where they want to live, so her brother's giving her the reception as his wedding present. He's decreed that it's to be a marquee on the lawn, and his word seems to be law.'

Kay had felt surprised that the normally self-assured air hostess she knew should allow herself to be so arrogantly dictated to on this uniquely personal matter. She was unaware of quite how sharply she had spoken until she felt Helen's eyes resting on her face with more than a hint of concern in them.

'Don't let Mervyn colour your entire outlook, Kay,' her sister admonished gently. 'All men aren't necessarily alike. I had ten wonderful years with John, and I wouldn't have missed a single one of them.'

'There's no comparison,' Kay answered tightly.

John had been the perfect husband and father, whom the fates had cruelly decreed should lose his life in a car crash, which still left his young son with a severe limp over twelve months later.

Mervyn was . . .

'An unmentionable.' Louise had forthrightly condemned the actor who was Kay's ex-fiancé, when she had prised from her the details of the broken engagement as they sat over a coffee in a nearby restaurant to which Kay had steered her, having no desire to pour out her personal history while standing on the edge of the pavement. Kay had shrugged resignedly, trying not to let the bitterness show.

'Mervyn lived in a zany sort of world. I never really fitted in. When a lead part came up in a West End play, there were two contenders, Mervyn and . . .' she had mentioned the name of an actor much further up the entertainment ladder than her then-fiancé. 'To make sure the scales came down in Mervyn's favour, he married the casting director's daughter instead of me. He got the part, and I made a swift exit.'

She had not told Louise that Mervyn had expected her to go on as before, and further, after he was married.

'Now I've got this part, Kay,' he had enthused, 'I'll be able to afford a little flat for us somewhere discreet, where we can . . .'

The stinging smack of Kay's small hand across his cheek was her swift—and final—answer to such an outrageous proposition, and a month later she had left her job as head buyer with Oliver Tait's famous hotel chain, and put London, with all its memories, behind her.

'I thought at one time that you and Oliver Tait might . . .' Louise had hazarded, but Kay had shook her head.

'Oliver's a dear, but he's a lot older that I am, and he's never really got over losing his wife.'

'Surely that was several years ago?'

'I know, but it affects people differently. My sister lost her husband suddenly. It happened within days of me splitting with Mervyn, and a combination of the two made us both sell up and leave London. With my experience as market buyer for the hotel chain, and Helen's domestic science training—she taught before she was married—we made an ideal team to set up a catering business. Oliver was very good. When a village bakery came up for sale, he let me go without too much protest. And now Helen and I have worked up a thriving catering business between us.'

Kay surveyed the kitchen with quiet pride, and reached for the pot to pour out another cup of tea for herself and Helen.

'I didn't mean to be quite so cutting,' she allowed. 'But Louise's brother does sound an overbearing type. I can't stand domineering men. Though to be fair, Louise is so pressed for time, she's glad to leave all the arrangements in his hands.'

'He must be generous to give her such a huge wedding reception,' Helen pointed out, but Kay refused to be impressed.

'He'll need to own a huge lawn to house his marquee,' she

predicted. 'And if he's really so generous, he should allow Louise to have whatever *she* wants, not what he thinks she ought to have. After all, it's Louise's wedding day. Anyway,' she shrugged, 'when he finds out what it's likely to cost him, I've no doubt he'll scale down the operation. He sounds like one of those types who've got pretensions to grandeur. His marquee on the lawn's probably nothing more than sheer swank. I expect it'll turn out to be the local flower show tent on the nearest paddock! And as for his guests, three hundred isn't all that surprising.'

'Numbers won't bother us so much if we can prepare the food beforehand and freeze it. Steer Louise's brother in that direction when you discuss the menus with him. I presume he'll have the final say as to what we provide, since he's paying for the reception?'

'From the impression I've gained of him, he'd probably have the final say in any case. I expect he'll have a menu already cut and dried. Probably à la carte,' Kay retorted darkly.

'We'll have to finalise something soon, with the wedding only six weeks away. It doesn't give us much time to plan it in with our other bookings.'

'I'm due to see York Demster on Sunday. Louise and her fiancé are flying out to Australia next week and they won't be back until the day before the wedding, so I've got to talk over the arrangements for the reception with her brother in any case.' Kay did her best to hide her dislike at the thought of the coming interview, and went on, 'Louise said she'd come and collect me at four o'clock. Her brother lives at Steeple Canon. It's one of those small villages on the other side of Wychwood. We haven't managed to penetrate that far yet.'

Since coming to the bakery, Kay had had little time in which to explore the lovely countryside around their new home. Since the tragic car crash, six-year-old Sam had steadfastly refused to ride in a car, and it had seemed selfish to indulge her own wish to explore, and leave her sister and the child on their own at home.

A clang from the old-fashioned doorbell brought her back to immediate necessities, and she jumped to her feet,

thrusting the unknown York Demster out of her mind.
'That'll be Vanda's husband, I expect,' she said, and made
for the front door. 'Let's help him to carry the things out to
the car.'

Two of Vanda's supper guests telephoned the next morning
to book early return parties, which meant Helen and Kay
having to work out menus for each, with none of the dishes
contained in the previous two.

On top of the work which they already had booked, it
kept them both extremely busy for the next few days, and
Kay had no time to give more than a passing thought to her
forthcoming meeting on Sunday with York Demster.

The day turned out to be bright and unseasonally warm,
and after they returned from church Helen took a deckchair
on to the lawn in front of the cottage, and announced her
intention to read the paper, and be thoroughly lazy.

Sam pleaded the opportunity to try out his new cricket
bat and stumps and, nothing loath, Kay changed into jeans
and a T-shirt, rubber-banded her shoulder-length bob into
a ponytail out of the way, and volunteered to bowl for her
nephew, cravenly using the close proximity of the cottage
windows as an excuse to use a soft tennis ball, instead of the
conventional, rock-hard sphere that Sam seemed to regard
as obligatory.

'Girls!' he jeered with six-year-old scorn for such
weakness, and demolished Kay's careful under-arm bowl-
ing with the proficiency of a budding professional.

'I've had ten goes,' he said magnanimously after a while.
'It's your turn to bat now.'

He rolled about with laugher at Kay's wild swings at the
ball. It was deliberate play-acting on her part, since she had
been keen on cricket at school, and had not lost the quick
eye and swift reaction of those early, halcyon days. But she
was careful to ration the amount of running about to which
Sam was subjected, although she hit some of his balls, since
the little boy was acutely observant, and she didn't want
him to suspect that she was pandering to his disability.

But inevitably the weight of his own small body on the
still newly knitted bones brought tiredness and pain, and at

the end of another ten minutes, the familiar pinched look
on the small face warned Kay that he had had enough for
the present.

'We'll have another game after lunch. I'm much too hot
to play any more right now,' she gasped, and at Sam's stout
protest that he could keep going for hours yet, she looked
across to Helen in a silent plea for support.

'It's lunchtime,' her sister said firmly, glancing at her
wrist watch. 'I've got a treat for us today. I made three extra
peach meringues while I was doing Vanda's order
yesterday, and I've got some ice cream left in the fridge. I
thought we'd bring our meal on to the lawn, and have a
picnic.'

She laughed as Sam abandoned cricket with a whoop,
and they were sitting round the remains of their feast when
a short hour later Louise opened the small wicket gate at the
end of the garden path, and hurried across to join them.

'We've finished,' Kay checked the air hostess's apology
at the intrusion. 'But I wasn't expecting you for a couple of
hours yet.'

'I'm in a tearing hurry,' Louise explained. 'There's been a
change of plan. We're flying out to Australia today, instead
of next week. Someone else is making a bid for the freight
line, and Dave wants to be on the spot to make sure we're
not gazumped.'

'I'll go and change right away.' Kay rose
accommodatingly.

'Come as you are, there's a love,' Louise begged
earnestly. 'I really am in the most desperate hurry. It's an
early evening flight, and minutes count.'

'If you're that pressed for time,' Kay relented. 'Just give
me a second to grab my jobs bag from the hall.'

The desperation in Louise's tone was reflected in the
speed of her driving along the narrow, winding lanes that
separated them from Steeple Canon and, recognising her
need to concentrate, Kay remained silent during the
journey.

Surreptitiously she pushed the end of a ballpoint back
through a hole in her jobs bag, which she held cradled in her
lap. It contained notebook, pens and calculator, plus wine

lists, and the various odds and ends that came in useful when discussing party provisions with a client. And it was irredeemably shabby.

She supposed she ought to buy another bag. This one was hardly calculated to impress prospective customers. But it had been with her on her first successful mission to a client, and she had conceived an affection for it, and was loath to part with it for that reason.

She leaned back in her seat, lifting her face to the sun, which combined with the wind to bring a becoming colour to her clear skin, and in what seemed to be all too short a time the tall spire of a church loomed out of the trees ahead, and a scatter of cottages announced they were reaching their destination.

Instead of slowing down as they approached the village, as Kay expected, the sports car winged straight through it.

'Hey, turn back! That was Steeple Canon,' Kay cried. Perhaps this was Louise's first visit to her brother's home, and she was not sure of the way?

'I know. York lives a couple of miles on the other side,' Louise answered, and kept her foot hard down on the accelerator.

There was only one road out of Steeple Canon village, and Kay could not recall any houses between it and the next village, five miles away, with the exception of a very small lodge standing guard beside an impressive pair of wrought-iron gates attached to large stone pillars. On the top of these, if her memory served her correctly, were a pair of superior-looking heraldic lions.

Surely Louise's brother did not live in the lodge? From what Kay could remember of it, seen in passing from the road, it had only a pocket-handkerchief-sized garden, certainly nothing large enough to contain a lawn capable of holding a marquee, let alone space for three hundred guests. The wrought-iron gates duly appeared as she remembered them, and to Kay's consternation Louise slowed down, and swung the nose of the car through them.

It *was* the lodge. She stared at the tiny building and its miniature garden with a frown, realising her worst impressions of the unknown York Demster.

'Thanks, Thomas,' Louise called, and smiled and waved to an elderly man who stepped out from the building to push the gates shut behind her, but instead of stopping she accelerated away again, along the smooth, beautifully maintained tarmac driveway, shaded by an imposing avenue of lime trees that were just beginning to show their tender young new season's green.

'But ... this is the driveway to Canon Court,' Kay stammered, taken aback.

'That's right,' Louise agreed cheerily. 'Didn't I tell you? York inherited it from Grand'mère a few years ago. He'd managed it for her for several years before that, and one way and another he's turned the estate into quite a going concern. He's into the breeding of pedigree cattle. He's worked up a good export business, so with York's cattle and our freight line we should be able to do business with one another,' she laughed.

Louise had *not* told her.

Kay knew the air hostess had a brother, and that was all. Up to now, their meetings at the airport restaurant—which Oliver Tait owned, and which drew Kay there on business and Louise for snatched meals in between flights—had been too rushed and too infrequent for more than brief everyday exchanges, and their mutual liking had never had time to develop into the close friendship that invited family confidences. If Kay had known that York Demster was the owner of Canon Court, and the local lord of the very large old manor, and its extensive estate, she would have taken the time to change into something very different from what she was wearing now, even if it had meant Louise missing her flight.

She sensed trouble when she first caught sight of him, as she swung out of the low sports car on to the gravelled sweep in front of Canon Court.

At the sound of the car's noisy exhaust, York Demster emerged from the house and strolled across the intervening lawn to greet his sister. He was elegant in faultlessly tailored, black lightweight trousers, and a short-sleeved, black silk shirt, with a vivid cravat knotted at the open neck, and he moved with a lithe, panther-like grace that

sent odd prickles over Kay's skin as she watched him
approach. His hair made shiny, jet waves above his high
forehead, and his eyes, Kay saw as he got closer, were as
black as the uncompromisingly straight brows that shel-
tered them. The former swept across Kay's slight figure
with a hard assessment, while the latter drew together in an
unmistakable frown of disapproval at what he saw, as
Louise introduced them.

'York, this is Kay. I told you about her.'

'Yes.'

The monosyllable was as curt as his glance was
condemning. It roved over Kay's beech-brown hair, that
the wind of their coming in Louise's open-topped car had
whipped from its rubber-banded ponytail into tiny tendrils
about her heart-shaped face, which was lit by pansy-brown
eyes, and an alluring dimple that came and went
uncertainly at the behest of her hesitant smile. Fervently,
Kay wished she had insisted that Louise wait while she
changed clothes before they set out, but her friend's
desperate plea had been persuasive. Which led her to
facing Louise's brother clad in clothes which, Kay saw with
a sinking heart, were creating quite the opposite impression
on her prospective client from what she had hoped for.

She winced under the hard grip of long brown fingers,
and inconsequentially her grandmother's long-forgotten
admonition flashed across her mind.

'Don't let a black dog sit on your shoulders.'

The black dog, a sturdy Rottweiler, was sitting at the
man's heels, but the same applied, Kay decided. York
Demster's frown was as off-putting as the stern, hard set of
his square jaw that oozed disapproval in every line.

In her confusion at the meeting, Kay had left her jobs bag
in the car, and had to go back to retrieve it. As she recrossed
the hall on her way back to join Louise and her brother in
the drawing-room, she became an unwilling eavesdropper
to the latter's efforts to force his sister to change her mind
about giving Kay the commission for her wedding
reception.

'You said I could choose whoever I liked to do the

catering for me,' Louise's voice was pointing out with asperity.

'I know I did, but . . .' York Demster made an obvious effort to force his voice to a conciliatory note, without much success, Kay thought tartly. 'I'm giving you your reception as a wedding present, sis. You don't need to spare the expense. You know that.'

'I know. But I want Kay to do the catering for me.'

'Kay!' The name came out like an explosion, and its owner's lips tightened as she walked towards the drawing-room door.

Unaware of her near proximity, York Demster continued with unflattering bluntness, 'I offer you the choice of any of the top-class caterers in London, and on the strength of a casual friendship, you plump for this chit of a girl who's a complete unknown in the catering world. From what I've seen of her, she looks as if she's playing truant from the local comprehensive school.'

'You're not being fair, York,' his sister protested. 'Kay's the same age as me. She just looks younger, because she's dressed in casuals.'

'Casuals? Is that what you call them?'

The sarcasm brought a rush of colour to Kay's cheeks, and perceptibly slowed her steps across the hall.

'Kay was head buyer for Oliver Tait's hotel chain,' Louise persisted. 'You know what a perfectionist Oliver is. The fact that she held on to such a job at all should tell you what her standards are like. And now she's started a catering business of her own, she's getting quite a reputation among the local villages, I believe.'

'Local villages. That just about sums up her capabilities, I imagine,' York Demster snorted. 'Instead of a first-class wedding reception, if you let your heart rule your head, and hire this girl to do the job for you, you'll end up with pub grub.'

'I heard that,' Kay said clearly, and with the light of battle gleaming in her soft brown eyes she marched through the drawing-room door to confront Louise's brother.

He fixed her with a steely look. 'In that case,' he said coolly, 'it'll save me the embarrassment of explaining to you why you can't take on Louise's wedding reception. It's out of the question,' he stated with flat finality.

He did not look in the least embarrassed.

Quite the reverse. His arrogant, unsmiling face, the proud carriage of his head, brushed Kay aside disdainfully, as if she was no more than an irritating insect. He turned back to his sister, ignoring Kay. 'Surely you can give me the name of one first-class caterer you're willing to commission to do your reception for you?'

'Oh, yes, I can,' Louise answered confidently.

'Then tell me?'

'Kay.'

'Really, Louise, you're being impossible! You always were stubborn, but . . .'

'Why? Because she refused to do exactly as you told her to?' Kay intervened tartly, and the man's eyes glittered.

'This is nothing whatever to do with you,' he snapped.

'As Louise asked me to do her wedding reception for her, it's got everything to do with me,' Kay retorted, and marvelled even as she spoke at her own temerity. 'It is *Louise's* wedding reception, after all,' she pointed out crisply. 'That gives her the right to choose whoever she pleases to do the catering for her.'

'It may have escaped your notice, but I'm giving her the reception.'

'It isn't a proper gift, if it's got strings attached.' Kay's scornful tone dismissed his generosity.

'Then what, may I ask, would you call it?'

'Moral blackmail,' Kay replied promptly. 'You're offering Louise a present with one hand, and taking away her right to choose it with the other.'

'And I've chosen Kay,' Louise reiterated. 'It's no use, York. You're outnumbered two to one. Give in gracefully,' she advised her brother with an unrepentant grin.

For a tense moment Kay thought York would put up a fight. His black eyes lanced into her own pansy-brown, with a look that made her feel unaccountably weak. Then with a shrug, he turned to his sister and said with disgust which he made no attempt to conceal, 'On your own head be it. If your reception's ruined, it'll be your own fault.'

'I'm in the business of catering for receptions, not ruining them,' Kay retorted sharply, and banished the flicker of unease that hoped she would be able to cater adequately for this one.

Louise gave a desperate glance at her watch.

'I'll have to leave you two to sort out the details between you. I must fly.'

'I'm ready.' Kay picked up her bag and scorned herself for the relief she felt at leaving York Demster behind. 'You can give me some idea of what you want in the way of food on our way home.'

'I shan't have time to backtrack, Kay. I've still got my packing to finish. York will take you home. You will, won't you, there's a dear?' she coaxed, and Kay's heart sank.

If she had known Louise would not be taking her back home, she would have come in their own van. Without thinking, she turned instinctively to look up at York, to see what his reaction was to being asked such a favour.

With a shock she saw that his black eyes were watching her closely. Were they reading her aversion to the prospect of riding with him? Perhaps even enjoying it? His heavy lids hooded his expression, leaving Kay unsure of what he felt about being pressured into spending his Sunday afternoon making a journey he had not planned, to take a girl he did not like back home.

Kay had no doubts about her own feelings in the matter. She would much prefer to walk, but home was nearly twelve miles away.

'Wish us luck,' Louise begged. 'I'll see you on the great day. Make me a nice wedding cake, won't you, Kay?' she begged a trifle wistfully, and Kay's eyebrows shot up.

She had assumed York would have already ordered the wedding cake. From the very best of bakers, of course. She concealed her surprise with a quick riposte.

'Any particular shape? How many tiers? And what colour?'

'Round, white, and three tiers,' Yord said promptly.

'Square, white, and two tiers,' Louise answered, and added cheerily, 'I leave the decorating to you. The bridesmaids are in sweet pea colours. The dresses are the only things I've had time to organise,' she finished ruefully.

Which should have warned Kay of what was to come.

'Square, white, and two tiers it shall be,' she promised, and deliberately did not look at York as Louise said, 'Don't forget, I'll expect you to be at the wedding as a guest, as well,' and quit the room with an airy wave.

Her brother followed in her wake to see his sister safely on her way, and as soon as he disappeared through the door, Kay sank limply on to a chair. With the catering to attend to on such a scale, she doubted if she would have time to be anybody's guest.

The next couple of hours with Louise's brother promised to be fraught ones, and she felt she needed the few minutes on her own in which to nerve herself to get through them. Her respite was over all too soon. She tensed as the noisy exhaust of the sports car, gradually growing fainter, announced Louise's departure.

And York's imminent return.

Now for it, Kay breathed silently.

He came through the outer door into the drawing-room at the same time as a white-haired, motherly-looking woman trundled a laden tea trolley through an inner door. They converged at a small table.

'Thank you, Bess. I'll lift the tray for you.'

York bent and took the heavy silver tray from the trolley with a courtesy to which the elderly woman seemed accustomed, because she left him to it and busied herself with shaking out a lacy cloth, on which she arranged plates of daintily cut sandwiches, and fluffy-looking scones, with a pot of what looked like home-made preserve, before quitting the room at York's smiling, 'We'll manage now, Bess, thank you. Miss Courtney will be mother.'

The glance he gave her as he said it made Kay feel quite the reverse of motherly.

His look made her tingle all over. She met the black eyes with a sense of shock. Smouldering fires lit their inky depths, that had been masked by his earlier anger, but now burned bright and brighter as they rested on her flushed face. They made her vividly conscious of York as a man, and not simply as Louise's brother. They made her acutely conscious of herself as a woman.

Without even trying, this man was rousing in her feelings she had not encountered even when she was engaged to Mervyn, and could not identify, let alone cope with, now. Disturbing feelings, that seemed to beckon her into uncharted territory and which, so far as she was concerned, were wholly unwelcome.

The brooding black eyes suggested that their owner might be an experienced navigator.

Kay hastily slid on to a chair on the opposite side of the tea table from him, glad of even the small expanse of lace table-cloth to act as a barrier between them, and wished fervently that she had insisted upon Louise taking her back home.

The air hostess's brother was potential dynamite!

There was no doubt he was well aware of the electric effect he had upon the opposite sex. The glint in his eye said he knew the effect he was having upon her now, and was deliberately stepping up the current simply for the pleasure of watching her squirm.

Was he trying this means of frightening her off, now that his earlier efforts to get rid of her had failed? Kay's determination hardened.

'Will you pour?' York said, and sat down opposite to Kay, and his demeanour turned the request into an order.

'Pour it yourself.' The words hovered on the very brink of her tongue, and it was only with an immense effort that she managed to bite them back.

'Bess made the scones herself, and the peaches in the preserve come from our own garden,' York remarked conversationally, handing Kay the plate with the careful attention of the perfect host. 'Bess is a splendid cook,' he added, and the words were a challenge.

If he expected a gauche boast that she could do better, he was due to be disappointed. Kay stepped warily round his trap, and to save herself from having to make an immediate reply she took a large bite of scone, and forced herself to chew it slowly.

When she could no longer help herself, she swallowed, and pronounced, 'Mmm. It's good. Very good.' Damning with faint praise. She knew a moment's guilt for the super, light offering.

But the food was no better than she and Helen provided daily for their clients, and she deliberately turned the conversation away from the contents of the table, and on to the purpose for which she had come.

'Have you got a menu in mind for the reception?' she asked.

Her crisp, businesslike, no-nonsense tone brought an unwilling tilt to the man's well-cut lips, but Kay was delving into her jobs bag for her notebook and ballpoint pen, and she did not notice.

'I suggest you draft out several menus, and price them, and we can meet in a week's time to discuss them,' York replied, rendering her show unnecessary. 'I'd like the marquee to be lined in sweet-pea coloured silk, to match the bridesmaids' dresses,' he went on evenly.

'The marquee?' Kay's head jerked up. 'Surely you've already . . .?'

'I've done nothing of the sort. I've got more than enough to do with my own work here, without taking on the nitty-gritty of a wedding reception. You've accepted the job, so it's up to you to carry out the arrangements. *All* of them,' he emphasised, holding Kay's startled eyes with a gimlet look that told her she could expect neither help nor encouragement from him. 'If the task's beyond you, say so now,' he suggested, with undisguised hope in his voice.

'Of course it isn't beyond me.'

Kay heard herself speak the words with a feeling of detached surprise.

First the wedding cake, and now the marquee! What other responsibility would this insufferable creature shift on to her shoulders next?

She was not left long in doubt.

In swift succession, York added to the list with remorseless satisfaction. Buffet tables. Crockery. Cutlery. Wineglasses. Garden furniture.

Kay wrote them all down in her notebook with fingers that began to feel as numb as her mind.

'Hire adequate staff to attend to the buffet tables,' York

instructed. 'My guests won't expect a self-service cafeteria,' he warned her with a steely look that brought a rush of colour to Kay's cheeks.

Her eyes flashed. York spoke as if she was not accustomed to catering for anything more upmarket than a village school bunfight.

'I didn't imagine they would,' she retorted, and wrote the items down on her pad with a ballpoint that suddenly shook, making her normally firm script appear as if it was written by an inky spider. She hoped she would be able to decipher what she had written when she returned home.

'Most of these things can be pressed into service for the ball in the evening as well,' York conceded, and Kay gritted her teeth in helpless silence, and kept her eyes glued to the rapidly filling page for fear he should see the growing dismay in them as the list continued unabated.

'I want a decent orchestra. They can play on the lawn in the afternoon, and double up at the ball later.'

'What about the bouquets for Louise and the brides-maids?' Kay asked faintly, and she was not being sarcastic. By now, she felt too punch-drunk to be anything at all.

'You needn't concern yourself with the bouquets,' York released her. 'They're being provided from the hothouses here.'

Kay crossed out the word 'bouquets' on her list with a relieved dash of her ballpoint. York's list of wants was going to cause her more than enough concern as it was, without adding the bouquets to it.

He tempered her relief somewhat, by offering her the choice of the hothouses for the flowers to decorate the marquee and the ballroom, but since he appeared to have plenty, and Kay loved flowers, she decided that part of the job would be a pleasure.

'Will you want champagne provided for the ball in the evening, as well as for the reception?' she remembered to ask.

York Demster would be certain to want champagne, of impeccable vintage.

'I'll provide the wine myself,' he told her adamantly. 'I'll choose it from my own cellars here, when I've decided on the final menu.'

Kay fixed him with a cold look. 'I'm quite capable of choosing the appropriate wine,' she informed him haughtily. 'I'm not the novice you seem to imagine. I was head buyer for Oliver Tait's hotel chain.'

'So Louise told me.' His expression remained inflexible.

'If you doubt my capabilities, why don't you ask Oliver Tait himself for a reference?' Kay flared, unable to conceal her indignation at his attitude. 'I've got his number here.'

She began to fumble in her bag for her notebook of numbers.

'I intend to,' York replied coolly, and Kay gasped, but before she could speak he went on, 'I don't need Oliver's number. He and I were at school together, and I know him quite well.'

'In that case, perhaps you'll be more inclined to believe what he says about me,' Kay ground out savagely, knowing she could rely on the highest recommendation from her ex-boss. She snapped her notebook shut decisively. 'That only leaves you to come and inspect our kitchens at the bakery, to make sure they're up to your expectations of hygiene,' she said with barely concealed sarcasm. She was stunned into silence when York retorted, 'I mean to do just that. In fact, I intend to do it this afternoon, before we take the matter of you catering for the reception any further. It was one of the reasons why I agreed to run you home.'

Did that mean he would otherwise have left her to find her own way back? Kay fumed.

And wondered what his other reasons might be.

CHAPTER TWO

THE MAN'S effrontery knew no bounds.

The voice of reason told Kay that she had no right to feel indignant. She and Helen invited all their clients to inspect their kitchens as a matter of course.

York Demster did not wait to be invited. He demanded an inspection as his right, and in a tone that said he would brook no refusal.

Kay walked with him, stiffly silent, to where his Range Rover was parked beside a low stable block adjacent to the house, and she climbed up into the passenger seat, nervously aware of his fingers gripping her arm to help her to board the high vehicle. Her arm felt red hot where he touched it, and the slanting glance that marked her instinctive recoil told her that he knew it, and scored up a minor victory against her.

York slammed the door firmly on her, and Kay had a sudden, suffocating sensation of being trapped as he slid behind the wheel beside her. Even in the roomy cab his presence was overpowering, and she felt an irrational sense of relief that the Rottweiler dog was coming with them. She would have preferred the animal to sit squarely between herself and its master. Without a buffer between them, Kay felt vulnerable, but York let the dog into the rear of the vehicle and fixed the steel guard rails between them, bidding the animal quietly, 'Lie, Glen.'

Without a second's hesitation, the dog lay obediently on the thick matting that had evidently been put there for its comfort.

The engine purred into life, and unexpectedly York turned the vehicle away from the main drive to the house.

'Where are you going?' Kay demanded sharply, and could have kicked herself for allowing the sudden qualm that assailed her to show.

'There's a back way out of the estate, through the home

farm. I might as well use the journey to drop off a spare shaft for one of the tractors that broke down yesterday.'

Was this his other reason for agreeing to run her home? Because he had to come out in any case, to deliver the spare part? A curious feeling, akin to disappointment, shafted through Kay, swiftly followed by astonishment at her own reaction.

The effect of this man was as swift as it was insidious. She had thought herself impervious to all men, since Mervyn. She determined to make sure that York got the message that he was no exception.

The home farm proved to be ten minutes' distance in the silent-running Range Rover. Ten stretched minutes, in which Kay tried without success to ignore the lean, tanned profile, so unnervingly close beside her.

Even when she turned her head to look out of the window on her side of the cab, she remained acutely aware of York. Of the strong, slender fingers that were relaxed on their hold on the wheel, but supremely competent as he swung the big vehicle into a sharp turn, and ran the gauntlet of a medley of barking dogs, farm machinery, and wildly flapping hens, before braking to a halt in front of a weatherbeaten farmhouse. He handed over the wanted shaft to the farmer, who strolled away towards the farm buildings with his burden, and his cheerful whistling followed them as York set the Range Rover rolling again.

Kay willed her eyes to take in her surroundings, thankful for the mental escape they afforded from her own inner tension, which she felt irritably certain York was aware of but did not share.

Determinedly, she fixed her eyes on the passing scenery. Spring had come early, and already the distant woods, noisy with nesting colonies of rooks, had their feet deep in an azure carpet of bluebells. Contented cattle grazed on the lush new grass, no doubt the pedigree herd Louise had spoken of.

Kay regarded them with growing interest. The animals' coats were glossy with wellbeing. Everywhere she looked, her eyes met evidence of sound and caring management. York Demster was patently not one of those landowners who was content to leave the management of his estate to an agent. Such obvious prosperity could stem from only one source: a caring, and hard-working, owner.

He spoke, and his deep voice sounded amused.

'Do you approve?' he asked.

Kay looked round at him, startled. She had not realised she had remained silent for so long. She did not attempt to misunderstand him. 'I don't know enough about cattle to approve or disapprove,' she admitted candidly. 'They just look good to me.'

It was a grudging admission. She had no wish to add to her companion's already inflated ego.

'They're the very best.'

It was no idle boast. It was not even a boast, Kay realised, surprised. It was a simple statement of fact, that accepted the sacrifice of years of effort in order to achieve a dream.

'Glen's been a great help,' York said, and at the sound of his name, the German cattle-dog gave an ecstatic wriggle. 'I daren't allow him in the hothouses, though. He's like a bull in a china shop among the pot plants.'

'The hothouses?' This was the second time he had mentioned them and, seeing Kay's interest, York enlarged.

'When an estate's main line is cattle, it pays to hedge your bets. One attack of foot-and-mouth disease can wipe out a herd, and the estate's main source of income, overnight. So we turned part of it over to horticulture, to be on the safe side. We suppply all the major florists hereabouts, and a lot of the big stores in London as well, with seasonal pot plants and cut flowers,' he continued.

He spoke with easy authority on the subject, unselfconsciously displaying a breadth of expertise in both of the cultures that held Kay's interest in spite of herself, so that the approaching cottage gate caught her by surprise.

Helen and Sam came out to meet them.

'Mr Demster's come to inspect the kitchens,' Kay announced briefly, the euphoria vanishing as she recalled the reason for York bringing her home. 'Meet my sister, Helen,' she introduced the two.

'Call me York,' he invited, smiling warmly at Helen as the two shook hands. 'It's much easier, as it appears we may be working together on my sister's wedding reception.'

May be working together. Not *will* be. Kay gritted her
teeth, while Helen smiled back pleasantly at their visitor
and said, 'This is my son, Sam.'

To Kay's surprise, York took the hand which the child
held out to him, and shook it gravely.

'Do you like cars, Sam?' he asked, seeing the boy's eyes
go to the Range Rover.

'No,' Sam said shortly and, tugging his hand free, he
turned his back on York and limped painfully back into the
cottage.

'I'm sorry,' Helen apologised, distressed. 'He's not
usually rude. He's got this thing about cars.'

York cut short her embarrassed explanations. 'Don't
worry. It's I who should apologise to Sam, for being so
tactless.'

Kay's eyes widened. It was difficult to imagine York
apologising to anyone, about anything.

'The kitchen's this way,' she said abruptly. The quicker
the inspection was over, the quicker he would be gone. The
strain of the afternoon hit Kay suddenly, and she knew a
great longing to slam the cottage door on the world in
general—and York Demster in particular—and collapse
into a chair, to try to marshal her disarrayed thoughts into
some kind of order.

She led the way through the cottage, nervily conscious of
York treading closely on her heels. Even with her back
turned to him, she could feel his eyes piercing her, and the
muscles of her shoulders tensed their awareness of him,
tightening into a hard knot that made her long to raise her
hand to massage it free, but she resisted the impulse
because he would see, and know he was the cause, and score
up another point against her.

She hoped in vain for Helen's support.

As they reached the foot of the small staircase leading off
the hall, her sister said, 'I'll go up and see if Sam's all right,'
and disappeared, leaving Kay on her own to show York
round.

'Come in,' she invited unnecessarily, as she snapped on
the kitchen light. Unnecessarily, because York was already

through the door, and pivoting slowly on his heel in the
centre of the room, his alert black eyes taking in every
detail of his surroundings.

Kay had no qualms about bringing him into the kitchen
unannounced. Where their work room was concerned, she
and Helen were perfectionists, and their equipment was
always kept clinically clean.

She remained by the doorway, leaning against one of the
worktops, and watched with barely concealed impatience
as York assessed the kitchen and its potential. His scrutiny
over, his eyes returned to rest with disconcerting directness
on Kay's face.

Her chin rose, and her soft brown gaze challenged him
silently, 'Find fault if you can.'

'It's nice, isn't it?' Helen remarked complacently,
coming through the door and cutting across the silent sabre-
rattling between them, and York's eyes unlocked themselves from Kay's and went to her sister. The feeling of
release was so potent that Kay found herself listening for
the clank of falling chains.

'I'm impressed,' he said, but he did not say in which way,
Kay noticed, although the smile he bent upon Helen looked
hopeful.

Kay stared at him, fascinated. The smile changed the
whole nature of his face. It wiped away the stern lines as if
they had never been, and brought the luminosity of verging
laughter to lighten the dark depths of his eyes, and made
him look years younger.

It also made him look devastatingly attractive.

It was obvious from Helen's next words that she was
already falling under his spell, Kay thought disgustedly.
'Stay and have a cup of tea with us before you go back,'
Helen invited. 'You can sample some of our handiwork.
I've made some cookies for tea.' Chatting easily, she led
York out of the kitchen towards the attractive little living-
room, cautioning him, 'Mind your head. The beams are low
over the doorway.'

'I'll put the kettle on,' Kay offered quickly, and was soon
pouring bubbling water into the homely brown crock
teapot, a far cry from the immaculate silver set on the

matching tray at Canon Court.

By the time she joined them, Helen and York were deep in amicable conversation, apparently at the greatest of ease in one another's company. York was saying, as if it really mattered to him. 'Was Sam all right, when you went upstairs?'

'Oh yes,' Helen replied easily. 'He's settled down with his paintbox.'

Which meant Sam was upset, and was working off his frustration by painting yet another picture of a swimming baths, Kay thought with quick depression, catching Helen's warning glance to say nothing in front of York.

'Will he ever lose his limp?'

The question was put with such genuine concern that it was impossible for Helen to be upset by it, and she answered without hesitation, 'We hope so, eventually. He'd stand a better chance if we could take him swimming, though. The doctors said that way his leg would get the exercise it needs, without it having to bear the weight of his body.'

'Don't you take him to the baths at Wychwood?' York accepted his cup of tea almost absent-mindedly from Kay.

A dash of milk, and no sugar. Would he even notice that she remembered? His quick nod of approval as he took a tentative sip told that he did, and she ticked up a point in her own favour.

'We're even,' she told herself with satisfaction, as Helen replied, 'Sam won't travel since the accident, so the baths at Wychwood are out of reach for him. Unfortunately the local cottage hospital hasn't got a therapeutic pool. They've got the land, but no money. So we're having to do the best we can.'

'So he has to make do with ordinary exercise?'

'Yes. But after he's been running about for a while, it makes his leg ache, so he has to stop. But we're persevering,' Helen said quietly. 'Kay's just brought him a cricket bat and a set of stumps. He's mad keen on cricket, and the running about helps. Kay had been playing with him when Louise called.'

Kay blessed her sister's quick perception that guessed

her mortification at having to meet a client dressed in jeans and a T-shirt, but if York registered the implicit apology, he gave no sign.

He nibbled a cookie, complimenting Helen, 'These are out of this world,' but refused another, excusing himself when she pressed. 'No, really. I've only just eaten.'

'I'll make some specially for you, at the wedding reception,' Helen promised, not ill-pleased with the flattery, and not for the first time Kay felt amazed by her gentle-natured sister's business acumen. After such a promise, it would be difficult for York to back out of the arrangement, and hire another caterer instead.

She found herself waiting with bated breath for him to speak. Would he choose this moment to tell Helen he was going to engage a London firm to do the job?

'Make sure to remind Kay to include the cookies in the menu suggestions she's going to draft up and discuss with me,' he said, and Kay let out her breath in a soundless hiss of fury that he still refused to finally commit himself.

York put down his cup, and rose to his feet, and said to Helen as if reluctantly, 'I must be going now. Thank you for the tea.' He turned to Kay, and his manner became brisk. 'How soon will you able to report results to me?'

As if she was an army private, reporting to her CO, Kay thought furiously, and resisted the temptation to salute sarcastically as she answered, with what she considered to be commendable restraint, 'I'll post our quote on to you. You'll get it by the end of the week, and you can phone me and let me know which menu you decide on.'

'I'd prefer to discuss them with you personally, and make a decision on the spot. Sunday would be the best day for me.'

He did not ask if it would be equally convenient to Kay. Arrogantly, he was giving her as little choice in the matter as he had given Louise about having the marquee on the lawn.

Kay clenched her teeth in an effort to stop the biting retort that rose to her lips as he went on, 'Bring the draft menus with you. In fact,' he added, and his lips curved upwards in a maddening tilt, 'it would be a good idea if you

came early, and cooked my Sunday lunch. My housekeeper
is away for the day. It's a good chance for you to show me
what you can do,' he taunted her slyly, adding, 'I'll pay for
the food, of course.'

Kay's mouth dropped open, but before her stunned mind
could formulate a retort, he was out of the front door, and
striding along the path to the wicket gate.

The Rottweiler greeted him with exuberant delight as he
climbed back into the Range Rover, and with a raised hand
and a grin in Kay's direction that mocked her simmering
rage, he was gone, and the bend of the lane hid him from
her sight.

'Of all the cheek!' she exploded, as she and Helen turned
away from the gate to go back indoors. 'For two pins
I'd——'

'Cook him the best lunch he's ever tasted in his life,' her
sister advised her sagely. 'It's a golden opportunity to net
one of the best clients we've ever had. And if we can bring
the job off to York's satisfaction, there's the possibility of
more to come.'

'He's arrogant beyond belief!' Kay raged.

Helen laughed, 'You've got to admire his opportunism.
No man likes being left to fend for himself for Sunday
lunch. You can't blame him for grabbing the chance when
it presented itself.'

'He could have gone out and got himself a pub lunch,'
Kay argued, unappeased. 'That's all he thinks we're
capable of providing, anyway.' Angrily she poured out the
events of the afternoon into her sister's attentive ears.

'Now's your chance to show him that we can do better,'
Helen returned, unmoved. 'We'll never have such a chance
again to prove our worth.'

The knowledge that Helen was right did nothing to
appease Kay, and she went to bed with the disgruntled
feeling that York had won her sister over to his side with a
humiliating ease that must have sent him back home to
Canon Court laughing his head off at their expense.

The next few days flew by on wings.

The daily market trip into Wychwood still had to be
coped with, as did the delivery of their various orders,

which involved making several journeys during any one day, clocking up the miles, and leaving Kay with only the evenings free to wrestle with the menus she had to prepare for next Sunday, to discuss with York.

The hiring of the orchestra and the marquee she tackled straight away, and was fortunate in finding both, and the necessary garden furniture, through one of her market contacts in Wychwood.

The staff to serve at the buffet tables presented her with more of a problem. They appeared to be as scarce—and as valuable—as gold-dust.

'Why did Louise have to pick the first week in June for her wedding?' she groaned, after the umpteenth telephone call had yielded the umpteenth refusal. 'Any week until then, there's staff aplenty just hanging about waiting for work, but the moment June sets in, it seems to start a veritable stampede to the altar, and there isn't a single chef or waitress to be had for the rest of that month.'

'Why don't you ask Oliver Tait for help?' Helen suggested. 'He told you to contact him if you ever needed anything.'

'He'll be in the middle of the wedding party season himself.'

'He may know of a retired chef who'd be willing to come back for the day.'

That was a possibility which Kay had not considered, and she reached for the telephone with returning optimism.

'Hurray!' she cheered minutes later, as she replaced the receiver. 'Oliver's going to check on his register of qualified stand-by staff, and book some of them for me.'

'How many?'

'I've told him three chefs, and six waitresses,' Kay replied, and Helen's eyes widened.

'*Three* chefs? Kay, you shouldn't!' Her sister's expression registered her consternation at such recklessness.

'Why not?' Kay returned hardily. 'York said his guests wouldn't expect a self-service cafeteria.' The remark still rankled. 'Anyway, I don't expect Oliver will charge him the top price. I told you, they're friends. Oliver said he'd received his wedding invitation in the post this morning. I

wonder York didn't expect me to send those out for him, as
well.'

'Just the same, three chefs . . .'

'With the menus I'm planning, I can't do with less.'

She worked assiduously on the menus for the rest of that
day, adding, discarding and amending until even to her
critical eye they were as perfect as she could make them. At
last, throwing down her pen wearily, she pushed the results
of her labours across the table to Helen.

'What do you think?' she wanted to know, with a tinge of
anxiety that she did her best to conceal.

Helen read through them with pursed lips. 'Caviare . . .
imported strawberries . . . I think these menus are fit for a
royal banquet!' she gasped.

'York seems to imagine he's some kind of royalty, so
that's how I've treated him,' Kay returned unrepentantly.
'You'll notice I've added the cookies you promised him, on
each menu,' she added with a sudden twinkle.

'I refuse to charge him for those.'

'All right. I'll put N/C against them,' Kay conceded
grudgingly. 'They're not too costly to make, anyway.'

'When this lot is priced up, a few hundred pounds one
way or the other won't make all that much difference.'

'No matter what it costs, it'll be cheaper than a top
London caterer would charge,' Kay pointed out with some
justification.

'A top London caterer wouldn't have been so wildly
extravagant.'

'So, York's getting more, for less. He can think himself
lucky.' Kay stubbornly refused to be moved. 'Now for his
Sunday lunch.' She pulled another sheet of paper towards
her. 'For two pins, I'd cook him the hottest curry he's ever
tasted.'

'Remember, you're on trial,' Helen warned.

Nervously, Kay felt as if she had already been
condemned, and was about to be executed, as she pulled to
a halt in front of Canon Court early the following Sunday
morning.

She should have felt more confident on this, her second
visit. She had chosen the outfit she wore with care, finally

deciding on a lightweight wool suit in a deep maize colour, with a natural, wild silk blouse, and an amber necklace and brooch as her only adornments. She could substitute an overall for the suit jacket while she was cooking in the kitchen.

Irrationally, she felt more nervous now that she was properly dressed than when she had first arrived in jeans and a T-shirt, but then she had had Louise to support her. Now, she was on her own, and desperately conscious of her aloneness.

She parked the van at the side of the house where she guessed the kitchen quarters must be situated, and was aware of York's presence even before he came into sight, approaching from the rear of the vehicle. She swung out of the van, and waited in silence as he came up to her.

He was dressed in jeans and a sweater himself, this morning. Working gear. Which reversed the position of their first encounter. She wondered if York noticed the irony, but he gave no sign that his initial assumption of supremacy was in any way dented. He took in Kay's neat outfit without comment, contenting himself with asking, 'Would you like help to carry in any of your things?'

'You can take this box for me, if you will. I'll bring the smaller one.'

Kay refused to enlighten him as to the contents. Let him wait until lunchtime to find out, and if he did not like what she had to offer, that was his hard luck. In a mood of defiance she had provided the wine herself, determined to make York see that she was just as capable as he was of providing wine as good as any that his own cellar could produce.

'I'll show you the kitchen and the dining-room, and leave you to it,' he said, as he led the way into the house. 'I check on the stock each Sunday morning, so I'll be out until one o'clock.'

Which meant that was the time he would expect his lunch to be ready.

He had not bothered to alter his own arrangements one iota so that he could discuss the menus with Kay during the course of the morning, and allow her to return home as soon as lunch was over, to enjoy the rest of her Sunday in peace.

He was autocratic, and inconsiderate, and . . .

With a scowl, Kay followed him inside. He led her along a seemingly endless corridor, through two doors, the second a baize one. There would have to be a baize door, she thought. York thrust it open with his foot and walked inside, to deposit his burden on to a marble-topped table.

He turned to relieve Kay of the box she was carrying, and placed it carefully beside its fellow.

'This is the kitchen you'll be working in,' he said, and waited for her reaction.

In vain, Kay tried to pretend to be unimpressed. The sheer size of the kitchen was overwhelming, for a private house, and the sensation of light almost dazzled her. Huge windows, with Venetian blinds that at the moment were rolled up to the ceiling out of the way, showed off to perfection the layout and equipment that would not have disgraced Oliver Tait's premier hotel.

By comparison, their own kitchen at the cottage paled into insignificance.

Kay took in the contents with amazed eyes. A bank of ovens was ranged against one wall, with huge canopies overhead to take away steam and cooking smells. Two fridges of commensurate size, and an equally large freezer, graced the opposite wall, and alongside them a veritable taxi-rank of heated trolleys was drawn up, ready to convey the food in mint condition straight to the dining-room.

The place was a chef's dream.

York broke through Kay's dazed silence. 'Will you manage to find your way round? That bank of switches on the wall over there controls each item of equipment. The switches are all clearly marked as to which does what.'

With an effort Kay dredged up her voice. 'It seems a large kitchen to cook for just one person,' she managed.

'Grand'mère used to entertain a good deal.'

Grand'mère must have entertained on a lavish scale, to need such a monster kitchen, Kay decided, but resolutely she schooled her expression to one of calm acceptance, refusing to be overawed by the magnificence of her surroundings, which was what York doubtless intended.

'Bess uses the small kitchen next to her own suite of rooms, in the other wing. It isn't worth opening up this one, with only Bess and myself living in the house. The rest of the staff come in on a daily basis from the village.'

So there was only York and the housekeeper, which meant he was not married. Which made him an even greater menace to the susceptible, Kay decided, and hastily cut short her train of thought.

'The dining-room?' she prompted, and York nodded.

'Follow me.'

He pivoted away from her, and silently Kay fell into line. His close-fitting denims hugged a lean waist, and hips that swung easily as he strode ahead of her, so that she had to trot to keep up with him.

The journey to the dining-room seemed to Kay to take for ever. They walked back along the corridor, through the baize door, through a varnished wooden door, and then another, before they eventually reached their destination.

Which explained the need for the heated trolleys, to prevent the food from congealing before it reached the table.

Surely there were other rooms in the house, closer to the kitchen? Kay thought impatiently, then knew immediately why this one had been chosen when York ushered her through the door.

Leaded bow windows looked out over a wide terrace, which was dotted with colourful clumps of low-growing alpines, blooming like patches of bright jewels between the irregularly laid stone. Gardens and lawns sloped away to meet the wide sweep of parkland, where yet more cattle grazed beneath ancient horse chestnuts already beginning to throw up their creamy candles of bloom. Sweet air flowed through an open window, and an unseen fountain tinkled an accompaniment to the spring chorus of bird-song.

'Bess has already laid the table,' York said.

Kay dragged her eyes away from the view. The table, she saw with surprise, was laid for two.

Bess was out, and Louise was in Australia, so who . . .?

York was not married. So was the second place laid for a girlfriend? Kay wondered curiously. York had not warned her that there would be a guest.

It was typical of his lack of consideration, she thought irritably. As it happened, she had brought more than enough food with her. She had catered for her own lunch as well. She had no intention of foregoing her midday meal, which she would eat in the kitchen, naturally. York would expect her to know her place.

She knew an impish regret that she had not thought to bring along a suitable cap and apron, to wait at his table as well, if only to satisfy her curiosity as to who his guest might be.

She pushed away the desire as unworthy, and York said, with a significant glance at his watch that was an open hint to her that she was delaying him from more important matters, 'I'll take you back to the kitchen before I go.'

'There's no need,' she told him independently. 'I can find my own way back.' He should see that she would be as glad to be rid of him, as he would be to be gone. 'Lunch will be ready at one,' she warned him, and added irresistibly, 'If you're late, the food will be spoiled.'

She turned away and marched to the door, but not before she caught the glint of silent mockery in York's eyes. With rapidly rising temper, Kay navigated her way back to the green baize door, but whatever her opinion of its owner, she could not help enjoying the facilities of his kitchen.

With the main course safely in the oven, and the starters and sweet in one of the fridges, she drank a leisurely cup of coffee before peeping into the freezer. What she discovered there wiped away any pleasure she might have felt in the rest of the kitchen.

She opened the door, expecting to find the freezer switched off, and empty. Instead, it was running, and boasted a modest stock of food inside. Astonished, Kay lifted out a packet of fish fingers, and discovered that the 'use by' date was a mere month ahead.

A rummage among the other packets beside it showed them all to have similar deadlines, and a frown marred Kay's forehead. Had York bought in the frozen food as a precaution, in case she lacked the courage to meet his challenge, and failed to turn up? Was there no end to the insults he was prepared to heap upon her?

As it grew closer to one o'clock, Kay found herself growing tense.

Would York be deliberately late for his meal? She would not put it past him. She herself was determined not to be, and at five minutes to the hour she discarded her overall, tied a gay apron round her waist, and loaded the first two courses on to an unheated trolley.

Cautiously she trundled her way along the corridor leading to the dining-room, timing herself to arrive at precisely one o'clock so as not to give York the slightest loophole for criticism.

The ancient grandfather clock chimed the hour as she pushed her burden through the door, and at first she thought the room was empty. She gave an angry exclamation. York had not come. He had done it on purpose, so that the food would spoil, and he could complain.

The muscles of her arms tensed to swing the trolley round and wheel it back to the kitchen, when York turned from where he had been half obscured by the long window curtains, and the angry words died unspoken on Kay's lips as the echo of the chimes died away, and he remarked, 'Punctual to the second.'

'Your guest isn't.' A second, searching glance round the room revealed that it was indeed empty except for York and herself. 'Will you wait, or will you start on your own meal? If you wait too long, the next course will spoil.'

He couldn't say she hadn't warned him if it did.

'We'll start right away.'

'We? But your guest . . .'

'She's already here.'

So it *was* a she! Carefully, Kay kept her eyes lowered as she placed a dish of chilled grapefruit on each place mat, and arranged salmon pâté and Melba toast in the centre of the table, for them to help themselves.

That done, she turned away to grasp the trolley handles again to trundle it out of the room, and as she did so she felt a brisk tug at the bow of her apron strings at her back. She spun round, grasping at the bright cotton piece as it began to slide from round her waist.

'What on earth do you think you're doing?' she snapped.

York was the last person she would have suspected of playing infantile practical jokes, and her already simmering temper spilled over as he neatly slid the apron from round her, and carefully folding it, dropped it on to a nearby easy chair.

'Sit down, and let's begin,' he said, and pulled out a chair for her.

'Sit down? Me?' Kay stammered, nonplussed by his unexpected move.

'Certainly, you.' York took her by the arm and steered her firmly on to the chair seat.

'But I thought ...' Limply, Kay sat, too astonished to resist.

'Surely you didn't imagine I intended to starve you?' Black eyebrows lifted in mocking enquiry. 'That would be too churlish,' their owner chided. 'And unwise,' he added with a lift to his lips. 'We've still got the menus to discuss, which should take us well into the afternoon.'

And it was not in York's own interest to waste his time discussing menus, or anything else, with someone whose alertness was diminished by hunger. His consideration was for his own benefit, and not for hers.

The table was a small one, just right for an intimate meal for two, but with York for company Kay would have preferred the classic music-hall version of aristocratic eating, with York marooned at one end of a huge expanse of polished wood, and herself safe yards away at the other.

Each time she looked up, she met his dark glance fixed on her, and read in it the same sulphurous mixture that had disturbed her the week before. Added to it now was an unmistakable challenge, and a watching kind of amusement like that of an indolent cat, biding its time before pouncing on the mouse.

Kay lowered her eyes to her dish, and dug her spoon into the chilled grapefruit, determined to let him see that he could not spoil her appetite. The astringent juice matched her mood and she finished the fruit. Then she nibbled her way through pâté and toast that she did not want, and which the curled-up nerve-ends that knotted her stomach threatened to eject.

York sipped his wine with a nod of approval, but to her chagrin did not comment on it, and the moment he had finished what he was eating, she pushed her chair back, and mumbled, 'I'll fetch the main course.'

He watched silently as she clattered the used dishes on to the trolley, defiantly tied her apron back round her waist, and escaped to the kitchen where she had another trolley waiting, and already loaded.

Flushed with the warmth from the oven, but calmer and more in control of herself after the brief respite, she returned to the dining-room and laid her offering on the table in front of York's critical gaze.

A deep serving-dish held a tender, honey-basted duckling, surrounded by small spicy sausages, and button mushrooms. To the accompaniment of an unnerving silence, Kay added other dishes, colourful with fresh new season's peas, glazed baby carrots, and new potatoes garnished with parsley butter.

A dish of orange salad sprinkled with a tangy dressing made its own bright contribution, and a round blue crock of pale apple sauce, and a darkly filled gravy boat, completed the table's festive look.

The smell alone was good enough to eat, Kay thought, and raised her eyes triumphantly to await York's acknowledgement.

He returned her look, pan-faced. 'This isn't a meal to offer a vegetarian,' he said.

'A *vegetarian*?' Kay stared at him, appalled. The thought had never crossed her mind. York was a cattle breeder, wasn't he? So how . . .? Suddenly, she felt sick.

She had racked her brains to find a foolproof menu for his lunch. Slaved for hours preparing it and cooking it to perfection. She had presented him with a gastronomic triumph. And he had rejected it out of hand, the second she put it on the table.

'You didn't tell me!' she accused him wildly.

'You should have asked.'

It was true. In a meal that was absolutely beyond criticism, York had unerringly put his finger on the one thing she had done wrong, and Kay had no defence against him.

He had deliberately allowed her to fall into his trap, and simply waited for the moment to pounce.

Kay drew in a harsh breath, hating him for what he had done.

'So it's a good job I'm not, isn't it?' he taunted and, picking up the knife, he began to carve.

Kay felt herself begin to tremble. Her head whirled, and rage burned through her like a fire. She wanted to pick up the precious dish of duckling and sausages and mushrooms, and hurl it into York's grinning face.

Hysterically, she wanted to laugh and cry, both at the same time.

'It looks out of this world,' York said, wielding the knife like an expert.

It was the same compliment he had paid to Helen's cookies. The tears nearly won, and Kay gulped and blinked, and found an extremely hot dinner-plate containing a generous portion of breast, thinly sliced and neatly arranged, thrust into her nerveless hands.

The heat of it stung her fingers, and she released it hurriedly on to her place mat.

'Peas?' York enquired mildly, and offered her the dish. Wordlessly Kay accepted one dish after another from him, and felt as if the first mouthful of food would choke her.

To her astonishment, when she forced a forkful through her lips, her own healthy appetite took over, and York's obvious enjoyment of his own meal did the rest.

Surreptitiously, Kay watched him eat, and knew a giddy sense of relief as he made steady inroads into the contents of his plate. He liked the duckling! Her choice had been the right one, after all. She had no qualms about her cooking. It was cordon bleu quality, and the realisation that York could not possibly fault the meal added to her own pleasure in the food, and released the tension that had threatened her ability to swallow it.

The fresh strawberry gâteau that followed elicited the

same surprised comment as the rest. He nodded approval of
the varied cheeseboard, with its accompanying bunch of
shiny black grapes and salted nuts, but declined to sample
its contents, protesting, 'After such a superb meal? I
couldn't.'

'You preferred what I gave you to fish fingers?' Kay dug
slyly. In spite of his praise of the meal, she still had not
forgiven him for the contents of the freezer.

'I see you've explored the freezer,' he remarked, latching
on to her wavelength without difficulty.

'There was no need for you to stock emergency rations,'
she told him resentfully. 'I'm not in the habit of letting
people down.'

His roar of laughter made her jump.

'They're emergency rations, but you're not the reason I
stocked them,' he grinned.

'Then what . . .?' Kay began stiffly.

'I always keep the makings of a quick meal that I can
rustle up for myself if I come in very late,' he explained,
controlling his amusement.

'How enterprising of you.'

She felt an absolute idiot for jumping to the wrong
conclusions, and she squirmed under the mockery in York's
lazy look that laughed at her firecracker, which had fizzled
out into nothing more than a damp squib.

'I'll give you the draft menus,' she said, and hurriedly
pulled them out of her jobs bag and passed them across the
table to him. The cost of them should wipe the smile from
his face, she told herself vindictively as she rose from her
chair. 'You can read through them, and my progress report,
while I clear away and wash up.'

She was in a quandary about what to do with the remains
of their feast, but she decided to leave it in the fridge for
Bess. If she took it home, it would be like eating the crumbs
from the rich man's table, and the prospect stuck in her
throat. As doubtless would the food, she decided with a
flash of humour, which disappeared as swiftly as it came, at
her next thought.

By making her sit down and eat lunch with him, York
had effectively prevented her from being able to charge

him for the meal. It was a galling situation to find herself in, no less so because she suspected he might have engineered it with just that end in mind.

Retreating to the kitchen, Kay expended her ire on the pots and pans, and amid the clatter she did not hear York's footsteps cross the non-slip floor, and come to a halt behind her.

'Are these ready to dry?' he enquired helpfully.

Kay spun round. To her astonishment, she saw that he had a clean cloth in his hands, and was reaching out to pick up the cutlery she had washed, and dropped on to the draining-board.

Her sudden movement almost unseated the dish she was holding in her hands.

'Why didn't you cough or something, instead of creeping up behind me like that?' she said crossly. 'You nearly made me drop this dish.'

With exaggerated care, she eased it down on to the draining-board, and turned back to the bowl of soapy water, washing and rinsing with urgent concentration. York stood behind her, and slightly to one side, picking up each dish as she put it down, and drying and stacking them neatly on the nearby worktop.

An unmistakable aura emanated from the man, dominating whatever situation he happened to be in. Kay could feel it beating against her, battering at her, and resolutely she steeled herself against it. But she could not restrain a small sigh of relief as she swilled the last bowl under the tap, and announced briskly, 'That's the lot. We can discuss the menus now.'

'I've already made my choice from them,' York announced calmly. 'I've ringed those items I'd like included from each menu. I'll add the wines to suit.'

How typical of him, not to accept one of her menus as it stood, Kay fumed. Doubtless he had chosen only those dishes which he, personally, liked to eat.

'You'll have to provide the beef yourself,' he went on with a slight quirk to his lips. 'My cattle are for breeding purposes only.'

So he had accepted the baron of beef. As well as her own

services to take on the reception, Kay thought, and was assailed by a disconcerting dizziness that was a measure of her need to win this job, and the strain the uncertainty had placed on her beforehand.

'Likewise the hams,' York continued. 'But the turkeys can be provided from one of our own farms. If you'll let me know how many birds you need, I'll have them plucked and dressed, and put in the fridge for when you want them.'

'I always choose my own supplies, personally. I'm particular about my provisions, and I only take the best.'

'Ours are the best. And you can choose them for yourself. That is, if you really want to?' He gave her a hard look.

'I do.'

It would give her the right of refusal, which she would enjoy exercising if the birds were not up to her own exacting standards. Kay decided she would be hypercritical when the time came to inspect the turkeys.

'I'll have them the week before the wedding, and put them in our fridge at the bakery.'

'I want the food for the reception to be prepared and stored in the kitchens here at the Court.'

Kay stared, momentarily rendered speechless with shock. It took two hard swallows before she regained her voice.

'What's the matter with our own kitchen?' she demanded indignantly. 'You saw it yourself. It's absolutely spotless.'

'I know that.' He cut short her tirade impatiently. 'It's a question of size, not hygiene. Your kitchen at the bakery is too small to cater for a reception of this size. You must see that.'

Kay did see, with disconcerting clarity. Equally clearly, she saw something else, just as unpalatable.

'If you want the food prepared and stored here, it'll mean I shall have to stay at Canon Court. I must be on the spot to receive deliveries ...' She broke off, dismayed by the prospect.

'That can easily be arranged.'

'From your point of view, maybe. But not from mine. It'll take two of us to cope with catering for three hundred people twice, and Helen can't travel because of Sam.'

'I'm sure you'll manage to divide the work between you, quite easily.'

York remained unmoved, and Kay glared at him furiously.

'What about our other clients?' It was typical of York's arrogance to imagine he had the sole right to their services.

'Have you taken on any more jobs for that particular week?' he responded swiftly, and there was an unmistakable hint of menace in his question that warned Kay he could yet change his mind, and hire another caterer.

'Well, no. Not yet,' she had to admit reluctantly.

She and Helen had indeed already discussed the matter, and decided to cross off that entire week in their work schedule, in order to concentrate solely on Louise's reception.

'Then that settles it,' York said briskly, making it clear that so far as he was concerned, the discussion was at an end. 'I'll get Bess to make a room ready for you, and there's a telephone in the kitchen, so you'll be able to liaise easily enough with Helen.'

'And you can wash your hands of the whole affair,' Kay said in a tight voice.

'Naturally. That's what I'm hiring you for,' York retorted. 'Now, come and have a look at the hothouses before you go home. You'll need to be able to find your way round them, to get flowers for decorating the marquee and the ballroom on the day.'

Before you go home . . .

He had no scruples about making it clear he was eager to be rid of her, and rescue what remained of his precious Sunday afternoon. Kay scowled. It was *her* free time she was giving up, as well as York's. To make sure he got the message, she said abruptly, 'I'll make it short. Helen and I don't usually work on a Sunday afternoon. We like to keep it for Sam, and this is the second Sunday he's missed out on.'

Contrarily, when they reached the glasshouses, Kay would have liked to linger in them for ever.

The Rottweiler accompanied them as far as the doors, but sat unprotesting at York's quiet, 'Stay, Glen,' as they walked on inside together.

The riot of colour under the shining glass brought a gasp of unrestrained delight from Kay's lips. It was like stepping straight from spring into mid-summer. Every conceivable kind of flower bloomed, from raised beds, from pots, and hanging baskets.

Perfume assailed her nostrils in a fragrant cloud, and instinctively Kay raised her arms as if to embrace the dazzling beauty of it all. 'It's paradise!' she gasped with shining eyes.

'I've told Luke you're to have whatever you choose to decorate the marquee and the ballroom.' York smiled and nodded to an elderly man busy among the flowers. 'He shouldn't be working on a Sunday, either, but it's his hobby as well as his job, and it's impossible to keep him away.'

'If it was my job, I should never want to leave it,' Kay enthused, and the smile remained to relax the stern lines of York's face at her unrestrained pleasure.

'There isn't time today to go through all the hothouses. There are more at the home farm. You'll be able to explore them all when you're here during the week before the wedding.'

Which meant she would be able to look through them without wasting York's time escorting her, Kay deduced. He spoke in an aside to the gardener, and turned her back along the aisle that led to the entrance door, and the waiting dog.

When they rejoined him, Glen was guarding a wicker skip, filled to the brim with flowers.

York bent and hooked long fingers under the handle, and swung it at his side, and the exotic sweetness of carnations tantalised Kay's nostrils as they walked back to the house together.

Her mind grappled with yet another facet of her many-sided companion. Most men would refuse to carry flowers, regarding it as effeminate. Not so York. He carried them with the same sublime confidence with which he did everything else, disregarding what other people might think of his actions.

His self-assurance was as arrogant as it was maddening.

And enviable, Kay acknowledged reluctantly. She found herself wondering if anything—or anybody—was capable of penetrating York's hard exterior, and if they did, what they would discover beneath it. She cast a speculative upwards look at York's face as she preceded him back into the house to retrieve her jobs bag, and caught her breath to discover his eyes upon her, holding her with his black glance which had been resting on her face for how long?

'What's the verdict?' he asked, with lifted brows, knowing it was he himself who occupied her thoughts.

'I . . . it . . .' Kay's cheeks flamed. 'I was thinking, I—I'd need at least six turkeys,' she improvised wildly. 'Depending on the size . . .'

She ground to a halt as twin devils of misbelief in York's eyes accused her of covering up. Accused her of lack of courage, for running away from the question, and dared her to answer it.

Bewilderedly, Kay did not know the answer herself. Even if she had the courage to tell him, she had not reached a verdict herself. Would she ever? The man was an enigma. An infuriating one. And one which she had not the slightest intention of trying to solve.

'I'll quote you again for the new menu you've chosen.' She took refuge in work, and turned quickly away from him to pick up her jobs bag.

'I haven't thanked you for my lunch, yet.'

Unhurriedly, York dropped the wicker skip of flowers on to a nearby chair, and with the same deceptive lack of haste, he reached out both his hands towards Kay.

Startled, she stepped backwards, away from him, but she was not quick enough to avoid his grasp. Before her heel had come down on to the floor behind her, she felt his fingers lock behind her back, preventing her escape.

'You must send me the bill,' he told her gravely, and pulled her towards him.

'No, I can't,' Kay stammered, trying ineffectually to pull away from him. 'I shared your lunch. Think of it as a—a—free sample,' she said jerkily.

'If you're giving away free samples . . .' he murmured, and smiled.

Wide-eyed, Kay caught the gleam of perfect teeth. She saw his dark head bend towards her. And then his lips closed over her own, sampling their sweetness with an appetite far in excess of that which he had shown for her excellent lunch.

Masterfully, his hands pressed her to him, stilling her convulsive attempt to break free and under the pressure of his kiss Kay felt herself grow numb. A strange lethargy took possession of her limbs, creeping through her body like an autumn mist, and freezing her mind, until all thought fled, and only sensation was left.

She could feel York's hands burning through the lightweight wool of her suit jacket, melting her resistance, while his lips made silent demands upon her mouth that were all the more frightening because they were unspoken.

The clean, astringent smell of expensive aftershave lotion mingled with the masculine odour of good tweed from his jacket, and the all-pervading sweetness of the carnations, and others in the skip she could not name, all combined in an intoxicating pot-pourri that threatened to ensnare her swimming senses.

An aeon of time passed before he released her. Or it could have been only a minute. Dazedly, Kay felt she would never know. For a long moment she remained transfixed, staring up at him, her lips still parted, and throbbing with the indelible imprint of his kiss.

A faint smile curved York's mouth as his hands released her, and reached behind him to recapture the wicker skip of flowers. He pressed it into Kay's arms with a mocking bow. 'Thanks for the lunch, Katie.'

Katie, Katie, give me your answer . . . No, that was Daisy, not Katie. And anyway, her name was Kay,

Her thoughts in a whirl, Kay grabbed her jobs bag, and more by luck than good judgement her fingers found the strap and slung it over her shoulder. Clutching the skip of flowers to her, she stumbled out to her waiting van, forcing her feet not to break into a run.

'I'll be in touch,' York called after her, but Kay did not turn her head.

She did not need to look behind her, to see his mocking

salute from the house steps, as she dived into the cab of the van as if it was a bolt hole, and slammed the door shut behind her.

A loud, grating protest from the gears measured the completeness of her confusion. Betraying it to York, she realised raggedly, and she let in the clutch and sent the vehicle kangarooing away from him along the drive, while her mind grappled with the astonishing revelation that the feelings Mervyn had aroused in her were mere milk and water compared to the sensations that coursed through her throbbing veins now.

Frightening, bewildering sensations, that exploded into clamorous life inside her, ignited by the torch of York's kiss.

CHAPTER THREE

THE DAYS that followed her visit to Canon Court did little to calm Kay's nerves.

'I'll be in touch,' York said. But when? And did he mean by telephone, or did he intend to come in person?

Kay jumped each time the telephone rang, and a knock on the cottage door had the effect of accelerating her pulse in a manner that made her impatient with herself and everybody else.

Scornfully she derided herself for her reaction, and managed to convince herself that it was occasioned by fear of losing the order for the reception, and not by York himself.

Wednesday came, and there was still no word from Canon Court, and the suspense made Kay nervous and irritable.

Her hands shook whenever anyone spoke to her, resulting in two dishes smashed to smithereens on the quarry floor of the kitchen, until at last Helen refused to allow her to handle anything that held precious food.

'What's happened to you since Sunday?' she asked, adding shrewdly, 'Or should I ask, what happened to you *during* Sunday?'

'I told you.' Kay bent to pick up the shards of the second dish from the floor, glad of the excuse to hide her expression from her sister, who watched her wielding dustpan and brush as if her life depended upon it.

When she had swept up the last of the spiky pieces, Helen said accusingly, 'I think you missed out the most interesting bits.'

Helen might suspect, but she could not know, and Kay had not the slightest intention of enlightening her.

'York Demster rattles me,' was all the explanation she allowed herself and, colouring furiously, she hurried out to the dustbin with the remnants of the latest disaster before

Helen could probe any further.

'Don't drop the wedding cake, or I'll sack you,' Helen warned severely when Kay returned after her cheeks had cooled, and settled down on the kitchen stool to put the first layer of icing on to the two large squares of cake.

They were rich and dark and fruity, a gastronomic indulgence, parcelled in home-made almond paste, and Kay wielded her spatula with an expert wrist, covering each with a blanket of glistening white.

At daily intervals she added two more thin coats of icing as the first ones dried, and she spent Saturday decorating the smooth result.

The slowly revolving turntable became a mesmeric thing, imprisoning her in its own demanding world, and Kay poured her heart into her work, losing herself in the creative artistry that was her greatest joy, and in the process she unconsciously found a release from the tension that had built up to explosive levels inside her.

The masterpiece which emerged at the end of the day impressed even Helen.

'It's beautiful, Kay,' she breathed. 'It's the best you've ever done. I can't wait for York to see it.'

'Don't show it to him, Helen. If he comes, and asks to see it, tell him it isn't finished yet, or—or—anything. But don't show it to him,' Kay begged nervously. 'If he sees it, he's bound to find fault with it, and want it all altered to suit himself.'

'He couldn't possibly find fault with that,' Helen protested. 'It's perfect.'

'Nothing's ever good enough for York Demster, except what he does himself,' Kay insisted. 'And I absolutely refuse to scrape off all that icing, and start again, just to please him.'

Under the implied threat that she would have to do the re-icing herself if York caught so much as a glimpse of the cake before the reception, Helen promised to store it out of sight, and Kay faced the prospect of a peaceful Sunday with a sigh of relief.

There was no danger of York coming tomorrow.

He seemed to value his own Sunday afternoon of freedom

as much as she and Helen did their own, and Kay had told him in no uncertain terms that they kept their day for Sam, so she woke up the next morning in the happy anticipation of her first Sunday in three weeks free from having to contend with Louise's autocratic brother.

Third time lucky applied, she decided with satisfaction.

The fine weather continued, even warmer than the previous weekend, and after lunch Kay joined Helen and Sam with a deckchair on the lawn, anticipating summer in a bright cotton print that bared her slender arms to the sun.

She was drowsing, with her eyes closed, when she heard Sam cry out excitedly, 'Here's a pony and trap coming!'

Ponies and traps were not uncommon in the village, but those that stopped at their own gate were. Subconsciously Kay registered the clip-clop of hooves approaching along the lane for some minutes before the sound ceased.

She opened her eyes curiously.

'It's a chestnut horse.' Sam aired his knowledge proudly.

'It's York,' Helen said, and looked across at Kay.

'He's got a dog with him!' Quickly Sam scrambled to his feet and limped as fast as his damaged leg would allow him to the gate.

Helen followed at a more leisurely pace to greet their visitor, but Kay remained standing where she was, feeling hot anger build up inside her.

In spite of what she had told him about not working on a Sunday afternoon, York had once again, arrogantly, disturbed the only free day she and Helen had during the whole of the week.

Did he imagine that because they had been hired to cater for Louise's wedding reception, it gave him the right to invade their privacy at any time he pleased? she asked herself furiously.

Through a blur of anger she heard Helen say, 'Hitch your reins over the fence, it's quite firm,' and Sam begged eagerly.

'Can I stroke him?'

Kay did not know whether the child meant the horse or the dog, but she herself had eyes for neither. Her stare riveted itself on York as he vaulted agilely from the large,

high-sided gig, followed by the Rottweiler. Fearlessly Sam
held out his hands, and Glen nuzzled the boy's fingers
amiably, establishing contact, but the chestnut mare was
too tall for him to reach.

Seeing his difficulty, York bent easily and swung Sam up
into his arms so that the child could stroke the mare's long
nose, with its attractive white blaze. Ingratiating himself
with Helen? Kay wondered sourly.

Why? Did he fancy her sister?

Helen must be several years older than York, but it was
not unknown for a younger man to desire an older woman.
Frustrated mother-longing, Kay thought scornfully. Un-
justly, because Helen was an attactive woman. But surely it
was too soon after John?

York knew about the car crash, because Helen had told
him herself. But it would be typical of his insensitive
behaviour if he chose to ignore it, Kay decided wrathfully,
and watched him with unwelcoming eyes as he returned
Sam to terra firma, and strolled towards her with the boy's
mother.

He came to a halt in front of Kay, and his black eyes
lanced downwards over her slight figure in its simple cotton
dress, sending goose-prickles over her skin in spite of the
warmth of the sun.

Kay stiffened defensively against them. 'The new menu's
in the post,' she said, taking up the cudgels without a
pretence of greeting.

'It came yesterday,' York nodded. 'It's fine, now.'

It had been fine before he saw fit to interfere with it, Kay
thought vexedly, but he was already turning away to speak
to Helen.

'It's such a lovely day, I thought I'd drive out and have a
picnic somewhere,' he said.

And Sunday being Bess's day off, he expected herself and
Helen to provide him with a picnic basket, Kay deduced.
The cheek of it! Her eyes sparkled angrily. She needed no
telling, now, why York had decided to honour them with a
visit.

What did he think they were, a transport café?

'We don't provide picnic food at a moment's notice,' she

began unhelpfully, ignoring Helen's urgent placating signals.

'Bess made up a hamper for me,' York replied, neatly defusing her rising temper. 'There's enough food in it for a regiment, so if you'd like to come along . . .? His eyes were on Helen as he gave the invitation, not on Kay.

'You and Kay go,' Helen said quickly. 'I won't, because . . .' Her anxious glance went to Sam.

'Is Glen coming, too?' Sam piped up suddenly, and the eyes of the three grown-ups homed in on his small, earnest face.

'Yes, he's coming,' York replied seriously. 'He sits in the front of the trap with me. If you want to come along, you could sit with me, too, and hold on to Glen's collar.'

Talking quietly to the boy, York turned, and began to walk back towards the trap, and to the astonishment of the two women, after a brief hesitation Sam limped after him, and allowed himself to be lifted into the vehicle and set between the man's knees.

The patient Rottweiler wriggled into his own accustomed position, and York took up the reins.

'York, I don't think . . .' Helen began anxiously, and hurried after her son to the trap.

'The man's out of his mind,' Kay muttered furiously, and marched after her sister, prepared to help Helen rescue Sam by force if necessary. The Rottweiler was the magnet which had enticed the child into the trap. Sam had always wanted a dog. But he did not realise what was about to happen to him, and when the trap started. . . .

Kay mounted the vehicle in furious haste, and took an urgent step towards the front, where Helen was trying to explain Sam's difficulty without making her protest too obvious to the child. Her sister might as well save her breath, Kay glowered. Helen was no match for York's arrogant self-assurance. He said, 'Let's try it, shall we?' and made a sharp clicking sound with his tongue, but Kay was too angry for its portent to register until the trap moved off, and then everything happened at once.

At York's signal, the pony trotted briskly away, the two-wheeled trap tilted at the sudden pull on the shafts, and Kay lost her balance, subsiding in an undignified heap on the hard wooden seat.

She clutched wildly at the guard rail to steady herself, her hands clenched tightly on the bar as she waited for Sam's scream to be let down out of the vehicle.

It did not come. Seconds passed, stretching into minutes, in which there was only the sound of York's voice talking to the boy, telling him how to drive the trap, and what he was doing with the reins.

Probably Sam was too frightened to speak, Kay thought tensely. The trap continued to bowl along at a spanking pace, and she burst out, unable to contain herself any longer, 'Don't go any farther. Take us back!'

For all the notice York took of her, she might not have spoken, although Kay felt angrily certain that he must have heard her.

She was less certain of what to do next. She tried to catch her sister's eye, but Helen's gaze was fixed anxiously upon her son. For the moment at any rate, Sam was quiet. But what if he suddenly panicked? Every second took them still further away from the cottage.

If Sam became hysterical, how were they to get him back home again? Like Helen, Kay dared not air her fears out loud in front of the child, in case she should precipitate an outburst. She could not see Sam from where she sat, only his two small hands, clenched tightly on the dog's leather collar.

She wanted to scream at York to turn round this instant, and take them home again, and then go away and leave them alone.

His voice droned on, explaining to Sam the intricacies of driving the trap, until Kay felt she had learned enough to grab the reins off him, and drive them back to the cottage herself.

Incredibly, for the moment at any rate, York seemed to be holding the child's attention, diverting his mind from the fact that he was once more riding in a vehicle, even if it was not actually a car.

But how long would it be before the novelty wore off, and reality, and panic, set in?

Just as Kay felt she would explode if she did not manage to get through to York, to make him turn the trap round and take them back home again before the worst happened, he turned the trap off the lane, and drew it to a halt beside the bank of a river, an ideal spot to hold a picnic.

And a daunting four miles, at least, away from the cottage.

York lifted Sam down. 'There's a lot of minnows in the river just here,' he told the boy. 'I used to come fishing for them, when I was about your age. I've brought along a net and a jam jar, in case you want to catch some.'

Kay gave him a vitriolic look. He had been so sure they would be prepared to fit in with his arrangements, and come along on the picnic, that he had brought equipment to amuse the boy. But her fury went unheeded as York turned away and spoke to the dog.

'Guard, Glen,' he commanded, and the Rottweiler obediently glued itself to the child's heels as Sam limped away excitedly towards the riverbank, clutching the net and the jam jar.

'Will here do?' York enquired, and without waiting for either Helen or Kay to answer he staked the pony, shook out a plaid rug on to the grass, and set a large picnic hamper beside it.

The quantity of food inside it made it patently obvious to Kay that it had been prepared for four, and as the meal progressed, her anger against York mounted.

Sam seemed calm enough at the moment. He had managed to catch a couple of minnows, which swam round and round the jam jar beside him, and he divided his attention between his hapless captives, and sharing his food with the more than willing dog.

'You mustn't, Sam,' Helen remonstrated as another half-scone disappeared in the animal's jaws, but York bade her quietly, 'Leave him alone. They're both enjoying themselves.'

That might be so now, Kay thought, but afterwards, when Sam became tired, it would be a very different story. She dreaded a resurrection of the tearful scenes that had followed the car crash. With time, and the move from

London, they had gradually become a thing of the past, but York's stupidity might very easily provoke a return, and she would not forgive him if that happened.

The melting pot of Kay's anger boiled over when, the tea finished, Sam and the Rottweiler trotted happily back to the riverbank, and Helen strolled behind them, keeping a cautious eye on both.

Kay's eyes were molten as she turned them on York.

'Why did you have to bring us so far?' she blazed. 'There were plenty of places along the lanes, where you could have stopped for your picnic. For that matter, why did you have to drag us along with you at all?'

Kay felt beyond caring that her attack might lose them the order for the wedding reception. Sam was more important than money, and they would get by without the order, the same as they had done before.

York turned from stowing the depleted hamper back into the trap.

'Relax, Katie,' he drawled, his eyes narrowing to watch her against the sun. 'Why so uptight?' he wanted to know. 'Let your hair down, and enjoy yourself. It's a picnic, not a penance.'

'It's all very well for you to talk,' Kay snapped. 'We'll be the ones to pay the penance, if Sam refuses to get back into the trap again. How on earth are we to get him home, if he does?'

'He showed no signs of distress on the way here. If he had, I'd have turned round, and taken him right back again.'

'It's a pity you didn't, anyhow,' Kay retorted. 'A short ride is one thing, but bringing us this far is crazy, when you know Sam won't travel.'

'All the more reason to get him started again,' York drawled, but there was a touch of steel in his tone, and it struck an answering flash of anger from Kay.

'I suppose you think you can walk in and work a miracle, just like that, where his mother and I have failed?' she cried scornfully. 'Or if he objects to going back in the trap, do you propose to ride roughshod over him, the same as you do with everyone else?'

York's jaw tightened. 'If Sam objects to riding back, I won't force him.'

'What, then? We've come at least four miles. Even you must see he can't possibly walk back so far.'

'I'll carry him home.'

'Carry Sam, *four miles*?' Kay cried incredulously. 'It would have been better if you hadn't meddled in the first place,' she blazed. 'Why couldn't you just leave well alone?'

'Leaving well alone is another definition of stagnation, Katie,' York told her lightly, and captured her waist with his arm.

Unobtrusively he had been moving closer to her while they argued. He had probably kept the argument going deliberately to distract her, Kay thought furiously, and jerked away from his touch.

But light though his hold was, it caught her firmly, and Kay found herself neatly trapped in the circle of his arm. Wildly, she twisted her head round to search for Helen, but her sister and the child, along with the dog, had disappeared among the trees.

'You're on your own, Katie,' York taunted, and Kay spun back to face him, her eyes snapping.

'Leave us alone!' she flared. 'Don't interfere in what you know nothing at all about.'

His touch was interfering with her breathing and her heartbeat; if she was not careful he would sense it, and discover more than was good for him about the effect he was having upon her.

'I can always learn,' he murmured provocatively, and with unhurried deliberation he commenced to take a lesson from her mouth.

Bemusedly, Kay wondered who was the teacher, and who was the pupil. Subtly, at the first touch of York's lips, their roles became reversed, and the soft, parted bow of Kay's mouth learned secrets it had never known before.

Dangerous, exciting secrets, that tantalisingly whispered of others yet to unfold, to those who had the courage to go in search of them.

Disturbing secrets, to which York's lingering kiss held the key.

His arm tightened round her, and the pressure on her mouth became more demanding, more intense.

'We saw a water rat, 'n Glen chased it, 'n . . . what are you doing, Aunty Kay?' Sam piped up from behind her.

'I . . . we . . .' Kay's cheeks flamed. She jerked herself free from York's arms, and his low, mocking laugh burned her ears to the same fiery glow as her face. 'I was saying thank you to Mr Demster for the picnic,' she blurted out confusedly. She was thankful Helen had not yet appeared from the trees, and wondered if her sister had witnessed the scene, and was deliberately delaying her reappearance so as not to embarrass them.

Kay could hardly feel more embarrassed, or more furious, than she was now. York's voice sang in her ears as he asked Sam casually, 'Would you like to hold the reins, and drive on the way home, Sam?'

Kay tensed, and then went limp with reaction at Sam's eager response. 'Ooh, can I?'

Helen strolled into view and came to join them, and they climbed back into the trap, with the Rottweiler, leaving Kay to follow on her own.

Men were all alike, she condemned them silently. Mervyn had wanted a mistress, as well as a wife. And now York was being all sweetness and light to Helen, and using herself, Kay, as someone to play with on the side.

Well, he could find himself another toy. Helen must do as she chose. She was more amenable, and with an altogether more placid nature, than herself. But York was to discover that sisters can be very different from one another, and she, Kay Courtney, would not be dallied with just as the whim suited him.

She was hired to cater for Louise's wedding, not to amuse her brother, so when she went to stay at Canon Court, he had better keep out of the kitchen, or he was likely to get his fingers burned in more ways than one!

In the weeks that followed, the cottage became a regular stopping place for the pony and trap, until Sam came to regard his hours with York's dog as his Sunday afternoon treat, supplanting the fascination of his cricket set, which now lay forgotten in his toy cupboard.

The persistent invasion kept Kay in a constant state of nervous tension, so that instead of looking forward to the weekends, she began to dread them.

York, when he came, paid her only moderate attention, and seemed to look upon her as a mere makeweight to the hilarious picnic parties, which he seemed to enjoy as much as Helen and the child.

He brought along another fishing-net, and he and Sam vied with one another as to who should catch the most minnows. The stream-fed pond in the cottage garden became a repository for the results of their angling competitions.

Helen, too, seemed to bloom under the influence of the carefree outings, and Kay watched the change in her sister with brooding eyes.

She would have liked to opt out of the excursions herself, but she knew that if she tried, it would bring an immediate and hurt protest from Helen and Sam. Worse, it would admit defeat to York, and so Kay gritted her teeth and endured the outings for the sake of her family.

'Sam's so much more confident,' Helen remarked happily as they returned from yet another outing. 'York's so patient with him, showing him how to drive the pony. I know it's not the same as getting him to ride in a car again. But at least it's a start.'

'What happens to Sam's confidence when York stops coming?' Kay anwered bluntly.

'Why should he stop coming? He seems to enjoy the outings as much as we do.'

'Because he's made it plain that we're not in his class as caterers, which means we're not in his class as people, either. That's why,' Kay retorted. 'He's simply using the outings as a sly means to supervise us until after the reception's over, and then . . .'

Her expressive hands spoke eloquently of what she knew must happen then.

'But Sam . . .' Helen protested.

'Sam's just novelty value, and nothing more. York's using him as an excuse to come to the cottage, that's all. He couldn't care less about how he'll let Sam down, when he stops coming.'

'You're prejudiced, because of Mervyn.'

'It isn't that.'

'It must be that. What else makes you so set against York? You talk about him as if he's got two horns and a tail.'

'So far as I'm concerned, he's equipped with a pitchfork as well!'

'Now you're talking nonsense. He's Louise's brother. He's nice, Kay. I like him a lot. Come to that,' Helen teased, 'I could fall for him myself. When you go to stay at Canon Court, you'll get to know him better, and you'll change your mind about him.'

'Not I. I'll stick to my cooking, which is what I'm going there for. At least it's predictable, which is more than you can say for men. I find their ingredients indigestible.'

As if to confirm Kay's fears, the following Sunday afternoon a groom arrived with the pony and trap, complete with the Rottweiler, with a message from York to say that he had been unavoidably delayed on a business trip.

'Some excuse,' Kay sneered. 'I told you he'd soon get tired of coming.' And felt her own sense of let-down turn to anger at the sight of Sam's disappointed face. The groom did his best, but he didn't have York's knack of interesting the child, and the picnic ended early, on a flat note.

Kay had still not forgiven York for his defection when she left the cottage a few days later, for her stay at Canon Court.

'He's probably given his housekeeper the week off, and he'll expect me to cook all his meals for him as well,' she predicted moodily as she left Helen and Sam waving goodbye at the wicket gate.

Contrary to her expectations, Bess was there to greet her when she arrived, and escort her to her room. 'Tell me if there's anything that isn't to your liking, Miss Courtney,' she urged kindly.

It was not to Kay's liking to be at Canon Court at all, but she could not blame Bess for that. And she could not complain about the accommodation that had been allotted to her, either, she decided reluctantly, exploring her surroundings with frank curiosity the moment the door closed behind the housekeeper.

After her own doll's-house-sized bedroom at the cottage, with its sloping eaves, and space for little more than a bed and a chair, this room was palatial.

It was a suite of rooms, she discovered, cautiously opening the two inner doors that led from the bedroom. The unaccustomed luxury did not make up for her being here, but at least it sweetened the pill, Kay decided, and settled for making the most of it while she could.

York was not in evidence when she went downstairs, and she assumed he was still making his morning rounds of the estate, so, adopting a no-nonsense attitude she politely declined Bess's rather wistful offer of assistance, and took possession of the large kitchen.

When York returned, he would see that she was here to work, and for nothing else, she decided firmly.

Soon the delivery vans began to arrive, as Kay had planned. The wheels she had set in motion during the previous busy weeks of telephoning now began to turn in earnest, and deliveries proceeded smoothly all the morning, until the bare store cupboards in the kitchen took on a festive air.

Still York did not put in an appearance, and Kay was busy stowing away the final delivery ordered for that day, when the kitchen telephone shrilled.

Immediately she stiffened. This must be York. He was probably summoning her for an audience, she thought tartly. She reached out her hand to pick up the receiver, conscious of the familiar tightening of her stomach muscles that his weekly visits to the cottage had done nothing to cure.

'Hello?' she said.

She had meant it to sound brisk and businesslike, and to put York in his place. Instead, her 'Hello?' came out wavering and uncertain, and Kay hated herself for having to swallow a quick uprush of nerves as she waited rigidly for his familiar voice to reply.

'Your lunch is set out in the dining-room, Miss Courtney,' Bess's rich country tones informed her. 'It's cold, with salad, so there's nothing to spoil if you're too busy to eat it right away. Let me know when you're ready for tea or coffee afterwards, and I'll bring it in for you.'

'Oh . . . oh, thank you, Bess.' For a second or two, Kay's mind refused to adjust and, aware of a surprised silence at the other end of the telephone, she pulled herself together with an effort, and added a hasty, 'It's very kind of you. I really didn't expect you to provide my meals for me.'

'You'll be busy enough, no doubt, without having the bother of cooking your own meals,' the housekeeper replied. 'Let me know about the tea or coffee.'

'I will,' Kay promised as she put down the receiver, and thought, 'That's what Louise will be saying, in a week's time.'

And hoped the high-spirited air hostess would not be fated to share her own bitter disillusionment.

Kay hesitated as she reached the dining-room door a short while later, and had to nerve herself to go inside, but she walked into an empty room, and saw that the table was laid for one.

She ate her solitary meal, piqued by the thought that York was deliberately keeping out of her way, in case she might make unwelcome demands upon his time.

'He needn't worry,' she muttered, not knowing whether to feel disgruntled or relieved by his absence as she carefully stacked the used crockery on the tray, and navigated her way to Bess's kitchen to save the older woman's legs.

'The meal was delicious,' she thanked the housekeeper. 'I'd enjoy my cup of tea even more if I could stay here with you and drink it.'

Bess's beam of pleasure told Kay she had said the right thing, and she had to steel herself to resist the older woman's reiterated offer to help her in the big kitchen.

'If you're going to spoil me with feasts like my lunch, you're giving me the best help possible,' she warded her off tactfully.

However kindly the offer was meant, Kay felt York's interference was more than enough for her to contend with.

The prospect that Bess might feel free to do the same would be the last straw.

She ate her dinner in the same solitude as lunch, and Bess's reserved, 'Mr York's out,' told Kay nothing, except that the housekeeper refused to discuss her employer's movements with an outsider.

Kay did not coincide with her elusive host until breakfast-time the next morning.

She was early, but York was before her, and said by way of greeting as soon as she entered the room, 'Have you settled in all right?' And before she had time to open her mouth to reply, he added, 'I've got an hour to spare immediately after breakfast. You can come with me and choose your turkeys. Ten minutes,' he cautioned her, draining his coffee-cup, and giving Kay just time to fly upstairs and collect her mac for protection against the steady rain that had begun to fall outside, spoiling the spell of fine weather that had lasted until now.

'I hope it stops by Saturday,' she groaned, turning up her mac collar as they made a dash across the gravel to the Range Rover.

Privately, Kay prayed the rain would stop long before Saturday. The suppliers were not able to deliver the marquee until Thursday afternoon, and it would be disastrous if the ground got a thorough soaking. If it did, it would not have time to dry out by Saturday morning, even under the marquee.

The worry remained as the rain increased to a downpour by the time they reached the farm where the turkeys were bred. The gum-booted farm manager accompanied them to the deep-littered barn where the birds were housed. They were well grown, Kay saw. Probably escapees from the Christmas festivities.

'Was it six you wanted, Miss Courtney?' the man enquired pleasantly, and at Kay's nod he said, 'Point out the ones you'd like. I'll separate them from the flock for you.'

It was not going to be as easy as Kay had thought. She hadn't really thought about it at all, except to determine in her own mind the approximate weight of the birds she would require.

She frowned as she looked at the turkeys. They were superb birds, beyond criticism, even to her exacting eyes. They clustered about the farm manager's boots, their lack of fear pointing to them being hand-fed. 'I'll need six big birds,' she said doubtfully.

But how to settle on any particular one, when the entire flock persisted in running round the farm manager's feet, gobbling in a demented fashion for the titbits that he scattered to entice them closer for Kay's inspection?

'I think, perhaps, that one . . . no, that one's bigger.' She halted indecisively, her eyes going from one to the other, unable to make up her mind.

She was uneasily conscious of York restraining his impatience beside her. Out of the corner of her eye she could see his foot begin to tap up and down on the sawdust, counting the seconds of delay.

To give herself time, Kay reached out a hand for some titbits from the farm manager, and held them out to the flock. Several of the larger turkeys, the ones nearest to the weight she was looking for, came boldly up to her and pecked the food from her palm.

'Choose the six you want, and let's get going,' York urged, and Kay turned a suddenly stricken face towards him.

'I c-can't,' she gulped.

'What do you mean, you can't? You insisted on coming yourself . . .'

'I know. But I didn't think . . . I don't know . . .'

She should not have fed the birds. Feeding them made a personal link between them, and she could not steel herself to point a finger at any individual bird, and seal its fate.

They clustered round her trustingly, and with a quick, frantic gesture she scattered the remaining food on the floor, and turned away, shuddering.

'I can't,' she whispered faintly.

What must York think of her cowardice?

What must his farm manager think?

Her eyes begged their understanding.

Dimly she became aware of a dog barking furiously from outside in the farmyard. The farm manager listened for a moment, and then when the dog did not quieten he said, 'I'd better go and see who's come. I'll be back in a minute or two, gaffer.'

York nodded. 'Go ahead. We'll wait here.'

The man strode away. A rush of cool air washed over Kay as the barn door opened, and then closed again quickly before the flock could make a bid for freedom, and Kay was left in the barn, alone with York.

She hardly dared to look at him, to face the withering scorn in his face that she knew must be there.

A gleam of watery sunshine glinted through a high window in the roof, making a rainbow of dust motes. Kay concentrated hard on the motes, trying to subdue the trembling that had taken hold of her limbs.

The silence stretched interminably between them.

York's voice sliced through it, harsh with condemnation at her squeamishness.

'You insisted on coming to choose the turkeys yourself.'

Kay swallowed. 'I know. But I hadn't seen the turkeys then. I hadn't fed them. I've never chosen meat on the hoof before,' she stammered miserably.

The meat she used always came neatly parcelled, almost ready for the oven, with little to link it with its living, breathing origins, which came trustingly to her feet, and took food from the palm of her hand.

'Now's the time to start.'

He reached out his hands and grasped her by the shoudlers, to turn her round again to face the flock.

Kay went rigid under his hold, resisting him with all her strength. Waves of shock pulsated from his fingers, sending the trembling from her limbs to course through the whole of her body, weakening her muscles so that she could not stand against him.

'You're shaking all over,' he discovered, and drew her towards him instead.

It was York, not the turkeys, who was making her shake. Kay could feel one of his thumbs working provocatively up and down her spine, sending tingles of awareness shooting through her.

Convulsively she arched herself away from it, but the movement only served to bring them even closer together, so close that she could feel York's hard length pressing against her, as unyielding as granite to her weakness.

'When Jim comes back, he'll expect you to tell him which six birds you want,' he reminded her uncompromisingly.

Kay's eyes flew up in shocked protest to meet his penetrating black stare.

'I can't choose them myself. I've told you . . .'

'You're the caterer.'

'Then I'll forget about the turkeys. I'll just have the beef and ham.'

'Turkey's stipulated on the menu.'

He was goading her. Deliberately driving her into a corner from which she could not escape, and Kay's resistance rose to match her temper.

'In that case, I'll change the menu.'

'If you do that, you'll break your contract with me.'

And then York would have the perfect excuse to dispense with her services, and hire the classy London caterer he had wanted in the first place.

Was this the reason he allowed her to choose the turkeys herself? Kay wondered furiously.

With hindsight, she realised bitterly that it was totally uncharacteristic of York to allow anyone but himself to make decisions. He must have guessed what her reaction would be when she came face to face with the living birds, and clutched at it as a means to snatch the commission from out of her grasp.

It was mean and cruel and despicable. And typical of York Demster, she fumed.

She glared up at him, but before she could give vent to the angry words that waited to tumble from her lips, York forestalled her.

'I'll choose the turkeys for you, at a price,' he offered smoothly.

Kay stared. Did he mean, at a reduced cost on her quotation for the menu? It was a way out of her difficulty.

But it was York's way. So what was the snag?

Without giving herself time to think, Kay snapped, 'How much?' and then she stopped.

The price was writ large in the black, smouldering challenge of York's eyes.

They offered her a way out of her dilemma. And dared her to take it. And the price had nothing to do with her quotation for Louise's wedding reception!

Kay caught her breath. She felt trapped, with her fate in the balance. Such a fine, delicate balance. And it was heavily weighted in York's favour.

'Send me a quotation,' she blurted, and twisted her face away to avoid a down payment.

'I prefer cash on the nail, Katie.' York bent his head over her.

Kay strained away, but he caught her to him, overcoming her puny resistance. She longed to lash out, to fight herself free, but her raised hands were trapped between herself and York, folded against the fine tweed of his jacket, and he pressed her to him so closely that not all her strength was sufficient to break them free.

His lips bored into her mouth, punishing her for wasting his time in bringing her to the farm, and the extra time he would be obliged to use in choosing the turkeys for her.

He did not allow her to escape a single second of the cost.

Kay's lips went numb under the onslaught of his kiss and, unable to move her body, she could only strain her head backwards to escape him, but all that her movement achieved was to bring the vulnerable slender column of her throat within his easier reach.

Before she could bring her chin down again, he took quick advantage of the offering.

His lips trailed slow fire from her chin to the wildly throbbing hollow at the base of her throat, laying siege to her senses, and a low moan broke from Kay's parted lips as she felt her embattled defences begin to sway under the attack.

Slight though it was, and instantly checked, York felt her momentary weakness, and his kiss changed and intensified, drawing deep with a deadly expertise to the untapped well of longing within her that Kay had only just discovered for herself, and had not dared as yet to plumb its depths, even in thought.

'Kay . . .' he murmured hoarsely.

'The missus has got a nice cup of tea ready, if the young lady would like to step across to the house, Mr York.'

The barn door opened, and the farm manager stepped inside and drew it closed behind him, and nodded across to Kay, 'I'll sort out six good-sized turkeys for you, miss,' he offered kindly, and rendered the price she had just paid to York totally unnecessary.

The interest on it still had to be paid.

At the first slight creak of the barn door, York had released her, but the fire of his kiss burned on fiercely in her veins, with undiminished heat. It was as if his lips had started a conflagration that nothing could extinguish.

Kay lashed herself with scorn that, after her experience with Mervyn, she should allow any man to set her alight. She despised herself for her instinctive response to York's powerful magnetism. She would not be so weak again, she vowed bitterly. If those were to be York's tactics, she would fight fire with fire, but it would be he, and not she, who would be burned.

Experience had taught her the hard way that, no matter how fierce the flames, eventually they would burn themselves out if they were denied fuel to feed on, and that she would deny them with all her strength.

Wretchedly, she wished she was a thousand miles away. York had not tried to hide his contempt for her behaviour, and the farm manager must be feeling the same way, although he managed to hide it better.

'Thank you,' she managed, and included the turkeys in her helpless gesture to the man's invitation. It was the nearest she could bring herself to an apology she would die rather than offer in front of York.

The farm manager cut her short. 'Don't think another thing about it, miss. I'll see to everything for you,' he said gallantly. 'You go along to the missus, now, and have your cup of tea.'

His offer of a restorative made Kay feel instantly worse.

It branded her as the hysterical outsider, too cowardly to take even the simplest preliminary steps to an oven-ready turkey. Kay cringed under the scorn that must be rife under the farm manager's kindly exterior.

She could not know how appealing she looked, standing there between the two men. Her cheeks were wearing a hectic flush, and her eyes glowed luminous, with a light in them that would have startled her had she looked in a mirror.

The farm manager's face softened into a smile. This girl looked like one of the pansies in his wife's garden, he thought, with an unaccustomed flash of poetry. With her big brown eyes and her sensitive face, dressed in a gold-coloured mac, too tender-hearted to pick out a turkey, she had the same delicate beauty as the flowers. She looked like a pansy that had been battered by a violent storm, and was just beginning to raise its head to the sunshine again.

'I'll take Miss Courtney across to the house, Jim,' York said, and foiled Kay's bid to escape him.

He seemed to know her every move by instinct, and always managed to be one step ahead to circumvent it, Kay thought resentfully. She walked stiffly beside him to the farmhouse, and then realised that if she had come alone, she would not have been able to find her way unaided to the door.

York ignored the two obvious entrances to the house, and led her instead along a narrow passageway beside an enlarged byre that acted as a garage. The walkway was not obvious at first glance, but it led to an extension of the house at the rear, in the one wall of which a door stood invitingly open, emitting a tempting smell of baking that rivalled that of their own kitchen in the cottage.

'Morning, Mrs Jim.' York ducked under the low lintel of the door, and greeted a woman who turned from the stove inside.

She was uncompromisingly plain, with a sturdy, muscular build not dissimilar to that of her husband. Her hands were large and capable, and looked as if they had never known the application of perfumed hand cream.

They were hands that would be entirely capable of

dealing with a turkey without flinching, if their owner wanted it for the oven. And Mrs Jim would probably be the one who would pluck and dress the six turkeys needed for the reception, Kay guessed intuitively.

The woman greeted York and nodded in a reserved manner towards Kay, her indeterminate blue gaze running over the slight figure of her unexpected visitor as she poured a strongly coloured brew from the enormous brown crock teapot resting on the top of the stove.

Contrary to her normal practice, Kay sugared her own cup liberally, and did, indeed, feel better as she crouched deep into a capacious wooden armchair beside the fire and sipped the scalding brew, trying to make herself as inconspicuous as possible.

Her companions made her feel totally inadequate.

The farm manager joined them, and helped himself to a large mugful of the tea, and Kay tried to shut her mind to what had probably been his occupation in the intervening minutes since she and York had left him in the barn.

The talk turned to farming matters, mercifully not turkeys, and the technicalities bandied between the two men were entirely above Kay's head, although the farm manager's wife joined in knowledgeably enough, and once or twice the men even deferred to her opinion, Kay noticed. None of them made any attempt to include Kay in the conversation, or to modify it to suit her. The woman took her own cup of tea to the scrubbed table in the middle of the kitchen, and carried on with her baking, leaving her visitor to fend for herself once her intitial duty of supplying Kay with tea was done.

Even the dog rejected her. A perky Jack Russell terrier trotted in from outside, gave Kay an enquiring look, then went to sit beside the table as being the more profitable spot from which to acquire a titbit.

But the puppy that followed it in made straight for Kay.

'Oh, isn't he sweet!' Kay abandoned her tea, and scooped the wriggling little body up on to her lap.

The puppy was warm, soft, and oddly comforting, in what Kay felt keenly to be a hostile environment. Her action was as pathetic as a child hugging a teddy bear, after being scolded by unfeeling grown-ups, she thought in self-derision, but the comfort remained nevertheless, and the small brown-and-white bundle playing with her fingers did more to restore her to normality than the tea had done.

'Mind your stockings, miss,' the farm manager's wife warned. 'The pup's claws are right sharp.'

'Never mind my stockings,' Kay replied carelessly. 'I can't miss the chance of holding him.'

'They're working dogs, not pets.' The words were repressive, and Kay glanced up at her hostess sharply, and surprised the beginnings of a smile on the homely face. It had taken an endangered stocking to discover a chink in the woman's armour, and impulsively Kay sought to widen it.

'What's his name?' she asked with a smile.

'He hasn't got one, except the one he's registered under. But we don't call him anything.'

The shutters were down again, and Kay's smile faded.

It would take a lifetime to get to know these people, she thought vexedly. She was accustomed to the easy, hail-fellow-well-met camaraderie of a constantly moving commercial population, and found this clannish closing of ranks against an outsider as repelling as it was obviously meant to be.

York spoke into the sudden silence that gripped the kitchen.

'Have you got rid of the litter yet, Jim?'

Got rid of . . .

Did he mean, in the same way as the turkeys? Kay's throat felt suddenly dry, and her fingers closed in an instinctively protective gesture around the puppy, that had by now tired of its play, and was settling to sleep in her lap.

'All except that one,' the farm manager replied laconically, and Kay felt sick.

How callous these people were, she thought with a shiver of revulsion. They were cold and unfeeling, breeding the unfortunate creatures, and then disposing of what did not suit their purpose, as carelessly as they would throw away unwanted vegetables on to a compost heap.

Just the same, in fact, as she herself disposed of waste

meat from her kitchen. The comparison was an uncomfortable one, and Kay jinked away from it.

To her relief at that moment York rose from his stool and said, 'We must be going. Thank you for the tea, Mrs Jim. Let me have the turkeys as soon as they're ready.'

'They'll be up at the house tonight, Mr York,' the woman promised.

Kay shut her ears to the conversation, and bent to place the puppy in a warm spot on the rug, wondering how long . . .

Without risking a backwards glance, she hurried out of the house beside York, but the moment the Range Rover was on the road again she burst out, unable to contain herself a moment longer, 'What will they do with the puppy? Drown it?'

She had to know. Plans to rescue it flitted through her mind, all of them totally impractical, because she and Helen could not possibly have a dog to live at the cottage, however much they wanted one.

'Drown it? Why on earth should they do that?' York's voice was openly impatient at such a question, but stubbornly Kay stuck to her guns.

'The farm manager said they'd got rid of the rest of the litter.' She ground to a halt at the implications.

'So he has,' York agreed. 'They've all gone to good homes. Jim doesn't go to the trouble of breeding Jack Russells merely to drown them.'

Of course. The farm manager's wife had said the pups were registered. Kay had forgotten. A dizzy sense of relief made her feel slightly light-headed, so that it was a second or two before she was able to take in the sense of York's next remark.

'If Jim hasn't already found a home for the last puppy, Sam might like it,' he said casually.

'At least if we had a dog, we'd give the creature a name.' Kay's voice was sharply critical, and York slanted her a keen look.

'They've got a good reason for not calling the pup by name,' he replied, as if, Kay thought, he considered she should have known what it was without asking.

'Tell me,' she invited. 'What's wrong with using the name it's been registered under?'

'Registered names are too long to be practical for everyday use. Animals need something short and sharp, which they can respond to. The bitch is called Gilly.'

'Then why not name the pup?' It seemed to Kay to be as senseless as it was uncaring.

'Because the pup's new owner might not like the name that's been chosen, and if it's given another one, it's bewildering for the animal. It's traumatic enough for a pup to be taken away from its mother and sent to a new home, without having to get used to a new name as well.'

Which put Kay firmly in her place as the ignoramus she was on the subject, she thought irritably, as York went on, 'When Jim brings the turkeys to the house tonight, I'll ask him if the puppy's spoken for.'

'Don't bother. We can't keep animals at the cottage.'

'I don't see why not. Sam likes dogs. He took to Glen immediately, just as you took to the pup.'

Kay bridled. She wished she had left the pup on the kitchen floor, and complained about the risk to her stockings, as Jim's wife had patently expected her to. With exaggerated patience she explained, 'We can't keep pets on the same premises as the catering business. The two simply don't mix, particularly in the eyes of our clients.'

'Surely you can keep the two separate, for Sam's sake? Every child needs a pet.'

'We could if we'd got separate premises for the kitchens, but we haven't, they're attached to the cottage. It's been a long, hard slog to build up the business, and we can't risk destroying the good will we've won, just for the sake of letting Sam keep a puppy. Keeping a roof over his head is more important in the long run. So don't interfere,' she warned York sharply. 'If you take the puppy to the cottage, and give it to Sam regardless, all you'll do is upset him when it has to be taken away again. Because my answer will still be no. And so will Helen's.'

She would ring Helen the moment she got back to the Court, and warn her of what had happened, Kay determined. If York persisted, he might succeed in driving a wedge between herself and Helen, and not only put her relationship with her sister in danger, but the business they had built up together as well. York had already interfered far too much in their private lives, and she had to put a stop to any more of his incursions before it was too late.

She could feel his opposition, like a solid wall between them, all the way back to the Court in the Range Rover. It made her own determination seem like a butterfly beating its wings helplessly against the strength of a window-pane, and she sensed that York would try to have his way over the puppy, no matter what she said.

The inflexible line of his jaw told Kay she had to move quickly and decisively to forestall him, because if York won this particular battle, who knew what might be the outcome of any further clash of wills between them?

CHAPTER FOUR

DINNER was a fraught meal.

Kay's mood was not helped by her telephone call to Helen immediately she and York arrived back at Canon Court. She used the kitchen phone to ensure her greater privacy, but her sister cut her short when she launched into her tale about the puppy.

'I'll have to go, Kay. Sam's got a fit of the miseries, and I can't get him to settle off to sleep. We can talk another time.'

With that, Kay had to let the matter rest. 'Kiss him goodnight for me,' she said, and put down the receiver with a frown. Sam had not had a fit of the miseries for a long time.

It was York's doing, Kay blamed him furiously. It must have been all the going out and about in the pony and trap, and then York sending the groom last Sunday instead of coming himself. It had thoroughly unsettled Sam, and this was the result.

'Are you satisfied, now you've upset everything Helen and I have tried to do for him?' She tackled York about it the moment Bess had served dinner, and left the room. 'We'd just managed to get Sam reasonably settled down, and now this has to happen. And it's all your fault. It takes him days to get over these bouts of depression.'

'Children get upset over all sorts of things.' York continued with his meal unmoved. 'It needn't necessarily be the outings in the pony and trap that have unsettled him. I don't see how something he enjoys so much could have anything but a good effect on him.'

'You wouldn't,' Kay retorted unforgivingly, and relapsed into glowering silence.

Coffee in the drawing-room afterwards did nothing to lighten the atmosphere between them. Kay curled up with a

77

magazine in a corner of the big chesterfield and pretended to read, while York took his cup to a writing-desk near the window, and began to work at a large ledger, on what looked as if they might be the farm accounts.

The rain had brought an early dusk, and he switched on a reading-lamp to illuminate the pages. The soft light brought the lean lines of his face into sharp focus. Against her will, Kay found her eyes drawn to him as he worked.

His dark head made a clear-cut silhouette between the light and the window as he wrote steadily, occasionally turning his head to refer to a clip of papers on the desk top beside him.

In spite of her dislike of him, Kay grudgingly had to acknowledge his attraction. It was the same sort of magnetism that would draw an early moth in through the open window, to flutter against the light of the reading-lamp, and it was this she was afraid Helen's softer nature might succumb to, if York turned his charm on her to try to persuade her to accept the puppy.

She could just imagine York suggesting, 'Try it, just for a day or two.'

And after a day or two, the animal would become a member of the family, and impossible to displace. And York would have ridden roughshod over her again, with the same infuriating ease with which he had done so all along. He had the same persistence—and the same thick skin—as a doorstep salesman, Kay thought bitingly.

He turned his head, and regarded her from across the room.

It was as if her angry thoughts had communicated themselves to him, disrupting his concentration on his work. His look was hard and implacable, impatient at her interruption, and resisting her thoughts.

His eyes in the lamplight looked as black as coals, and they shone diamond-bright, with a sharp glitter in them that surely the lamplight was too soft to bring out with such intensity?

Kay tried to look away, and found she could not.

York's look held her, like a rabbit fascinated by a snake,

terrified, and yet drawn by a fearful magnetism that it was unable to resist. Instinctively she shrank back deeper into the thick cushions of the chesterfield, and York's eyes flickered in response to her tacit withdrawal.

Fluidly, he rose to his feet, his eyes still holding her enchained. He came towards her with a silent stride. One more step, and he would be standing over her. His foot rose to take it just as the hall telephone rang.

York paused and turned his head, and the chain was broken. The phone rang again, shrilly demanding, and he turned abruptly on his heel and went to answer it, shutting the door behind him.

Kay flicked her tongue across lips that had gone suddenly dry, and felt the cold clamminess of sweat on the palms of her hands.

He was a long time answering the telephone.

Kay could hear his voice, the words muffled by the thick door, and eventually the sharp click of the receiver being replaced. She tensed against his return, but then his voice came again. The telephone had not rung, so he must be making a call of his own.

Superimposing itself on the one-sided conversation, the sound of a car engine reached Kay's ears faintly from outside. It was probably the farm manager with the turkeys. Kay started to get up, and then resumed her seat. If the man had brought the turkeys, it was up to York to come and tell her so, not for her to go in search of him.

Stubbornly she remained where she was. She heard the receiver click down again, and although she listened, there were no more calls. After what seemed to Kay a long time, she heard the car depart.

Still York did not return to the drawing-room. Half an hour passed, and then another half-hour, agonisingly slowly, and at last Kay gave up and began to wander restlessly about the room.

Was York intending to remain away for the whole of the rest of the evening?

She did not want his company. But perversely, neither did she want her own. She resented him going off without a

word of explanation. He did not owe her one, but
nevertheless it would not have hurt him to pop his head
round the door and tell her he wouldn't be back for a while,
she thought resentfully.

A quick twirl of the switches on the television set offered
nothing that attracted her, and she found herself missing
the cosy company of Helen and Sam at the cottage. The
Rottweiler would have been a help, but he had gone out of
the room with York, and must be still with him. Wherever
that was.

In desperation Kay turned to the bookcase for distraction, and unearthed a surprising and varied selection of
reading matter. Surely the volumes of poetry must have
belonged to Grand'mère? But no, on closer inspection she
discovered they were modern prints, which bore York's
name on the flyleaf. Kay took one back to the fire, and
began to read curiously.

She had not expected to share this mutual pleasure with
York, but the well-thumbed anthology pointed to hours of
leisured enjoyment equal to her own, and she was soon lost
among the pages.

She was roused from her absorption as the sonorous
chimes of the grandfather clock reached ten. Surprised, she
checked her wrist-watch, and saw that she had not
miscounted.

York had not come back.

She did not know for sure if the turkeys had come, either,
she remembered. The car engine she heard need not
necessarily have belonged to the farm manager. To satisfy
herself, she went into the big kitchen to check the freezer.

Neither it nor the fridge boasted turkeys, and Kay knew
a slight satisfaction that even the capable Mrs Jim must
have over-estimated her ability to cope with the plucking
and dressing of six birds in the time she had so confidently
promised.

She did not see York again that evening. At eleven
o'clock she went to bed, still angry with him for
disappearing without saying he was going out. And even
angrier with herself for letting the omission matter.

The birds had still not arrived by the following lunchtime, and Kay began to get anxious.

'I can't wait for ever,' she told York crisply when he came in for his meal. 'It's already Wednesday, and there are six birds to be prepared and stuffed and cooked, and only just over two days left to do it all in.'

'Relax, Katie,' he drawled, and Kay stiffened.

She wished he would not keep telling her to relax. It was the last thing she felt remotely capable of doing in his company, although Helen seemed to manage it easily enough.

'The turkeys came last night,' he informed her.

'They're not in the fridge. At least, not in the big kitchen.'

'I took them to Helen. She's probably got a couple of them cooked already.'

'You ... *what*?'

That was where York had gone after dinner last night! He had been to the cottage to see Helen and Sam, with never a word to herself beforehand. With never an offer to take her with him.

Kay choked on an uprush of anger. Was there no end to the mischief York could cause in her personal life? Once again, without bothering to consult her first, he had interfered, and overturned all her own and Helen's careful plans on how to divide the work of the wedding reception between them.

'You said you wanted the cooking done at Canon Court,' she gravelled at last, through clenched teeth.

'I've changed my mind.'

'Helen can't manage the birds. She's doing the trifles and ...'

'She *was* doing the trifles. You're doing them now.'

York was not only interfering, he was giving her orders. It was insufferable. *He* was insufferable.

Kay felt an irresistible urge to throw things—hard, heavy things, and all of them at York! She clenched her hands so tightly that her fingernails dug into her palms as she fought for self-control.

'I suppose you took the puppy with you, as well as the turkeys?' she managed at last in a strangled voice.

'No,' York denied gravely. 'Although I did mention it to Helen. Out of Sam's hearing, of course.'

'Oh, of *course*. What did Helen say?'

If Helen had meekly allowed herself to be steam-rollered into accepting the puppy after all their earlier joint discussions on the subject and their firm decision not to allow animals at the cottage, she would . . . she would walk out of the whole affair, including the wedding reception, Kay fumed.

'Helen said she'd think about it. So we left it at that.'

Too right she'll think about it! Kay vowed darkly. Think of a dozen different ways to say no, and make York accept each one of them for an answer.

Out loud she claimed hotly, 'Sam's quite miserable enough as it is, without being upset any further. Helen told me on the phone . . .'

'Yes, he was a bit steamed up,' York admitted. 'He'd got all his sums wrong at school. But he was all right before I came home.'

'His sums?' Kay echoed. She felt taken aback.

'He'd been given some new sums he'd never done before,' York explained. 'When Helen showed me his book, I realised he'd made the same mistake all through. I went upstairs and explained it to him, and when he saw what he'd been doing wrong he did them all again in no time, and got them right, to take back to his teacher tomorrow. He was asleep almost before I got downstairs again.'

'Oh, *magic*.' Kay's voice was loaded with venom. 'Mr Fixit does it again.'

'Would you have preferred me to let Sam cry himself to sleep?' There was steel in York's voice to match the venom.

'No, of course not.'

But Kay felt she would have preferred it to be anyone—anyone else on earth—to guide Sam through his sums, rather than York.

Their next passage-at-arms came about over the powder-room.

It was on the list of amenities to be made available to the wedding guests on Saturday, and Kay chose a small cloakroom that led off from the lawn where the marquee was to be erected.

'It'll be ideal for the purpose,' she decided, and asked York for the key when she discovered that the toilets leading off it were locked.

'Forget the powder-room,' he said. 'Bess will do it.'

'Forget it?' Kay stared her astonishment. 'But you wanted a powder-room made ready for the ladies. It's on my list of things to do.' She waved the paper crossly in front of him.'

'I know.'

'Don't tell me you've changed your mind about something else?'

Kay's eyes snapped. First it was the wine, then the turkeys. Now it was the powder-room.

'Don't you trust me to do *anything*? Perhaps you'd like Bess to do the trifles, as well? If so, I might as well give up and go home, because all the rest is already finished, and in the freezer.'

She smarted under York's restriction as if he had physically slapped her down.

'I've no doubt Bess would like to do the trifles. But she hasn't got the energy any more,' York replied evenly, and swept on before Kay could butt in, 'She's feeling it very keenly, not being able to do Louise's wedding reception herself. She always used to be in charge of all the catering arrangements at Grand'mère's parties, but she's simply past it now. Which is why I want her to do the powder-room herself. The house is Bess's bailiwick,' he warned Kay, and his tone was hard, emphasising her position as an outsider. 'I won't allow my housekeeper to feel she's being pushed out,' he said sternly.

With that, Kay could not argue. But it did not excuse his attitude about the wine, or the turkeys.

For the first time since she had come to Canon Court, Kay did not ring Helen that evening. She felt that if she did, she might say more than she intended, and what she feared might well happen—York would have succeeded in driving a wedge between herself and her sister, as well as interfering in their business.

He had a lot to account for, Kay told herself blackly as she tackled the unasked-for task of gathering ingredients for the trifles.

As the days ticked by, the pace of the work increased. By Wednesday morning the rain had stopped, and on Thursday afternoon the marquee arrived, complete with its gang of erectors.

They had just completed their task when York returned from a visit to one of the outlying farms, and Kay's heart sank. So much for her hope that he would not appear until after the suppliers' men had left.

'It's too late to change the marquee now.' She took the offensive before York had an opportunity to comment on the massive structure that took up half the lawn. It included a wide roof canopy connected to the house, and looked an altogether impressive sight, she thought.

'It looks perfect to me.' York's reply stunned her, and before she could get her breath back he added, with a quirk of one eyebrow that jeered at her open astonishment, 'Even to my untutored eyes, I'd say the lining looks an exact match to the bridesmaids' dresses.'

The huge marquee was lined from floor to roof in wide stripes of ruched silk, in every imaginable sweet-pea shade, and Kay gasped with delight at the sight of it, and gasped again in sheer disbelief at York's unqualified approval.

He's softening, she thought incredulously, but knew by the look he slanted at her as he turned to speak to the foreman that he was doing nothing of the sort.

Louise went into raptures of delight when she and Dave arrived the next morning, and declared, 'The marquee will outshine the bridesmaids!' And thereby restored Kay's ego somewhat, as she busied herself in the hothouses, choosing flowers for her final task of decorating the marquee.

Fortunately the day started cool, and she left the job until the very last minute so that the flowers would remain mint-fresh. She was glad to have something to occupy herself that would take her out of the house after their early dinner that evening.

The two young bridesmaids, Dave's nieces, arrived with their parents during the afternoon, and the meal was brought forward to suit their bedtime. It was very much a family gathering, and Kay felt even more of an outsider than she had done before.

The moment the meal was over, she pleaded work to do, and escaped to the marquee.

Dusk was falling by the time she pressed the last blooms into the arrangements, and stood back to survey the results of her handiwork.

Long buffet tables gleamed snowily along one entire side of the marquee, backed by banks of flowers in enormous pottery urns, contrasting with the low posy bowls on the tables themselves, which Kay had added to give colour without getting in the way of the food.

On the other side of the marquee, a table had been placed ready to hold the wedding cake, and beside it, where the bride and groom were to stand to receive their guests, Kay had built her *pièce de résistance*, a bower of sweet peas and roses.

Under her hands, the marquee had been transformed into an extravagance of colour and perfume and, weary though she was, Kay felt well satisfied with the results of her labours. If York did not like it, she thought thankfully, it was too late for him to do anything about it now.

She felt him come up behind her, walking without sound on the soft grass.

Her mind told her that she was alone in the marquee, but her senses knew differently. They reacted like the sensitive antennae of a radar probe, picking up the unmistakable electric impulses that vibrated from York's presence, homing in on her nerve endings with a deadly accuracy that set them jangling in response.

With an effort that promised a stiff neck on the morrow, Kay held herself rigid, and refused to turn her head to acknowledge him. Instead, defiantly, she tilted it to one side, pretending to be considering the bower. But her ploy was rendered pointless when he followed her. His hands came out to rest lightly on her shoulders, and nervous reaction made her start violently, and a thorn from one of the roses dug into her fingers, drawing a drop of blood.

Instinctively she jerked her hand away from the pain, and her quick backwards step brought her hard up against York's unyielding frame.

'Did it break the skin? Poor Katie,' he mocked, as she sucked her abused finger.

The prick stung as if York himself had got under her skin, digging deep to penetrate the barrier of self-preservation which she had carefully erected since Mervyn.

His voice, close in her ear, made a warm fan of breath across her face, soft and evocative, and Kay made a convulsive movement away from him.

Immediately his hands on her shoulders tightened their grip, drawing her back to her former position against him. 'Why so edgy?' he enquired lightly. 'Did I frighten you?'

His touch was frightening her, for reasons she did not want to think about.

'No . . . yes . . .' Kay wished he would loose her, so that she could move farther away from him. The long, close contact of his body was warm against her back, which seemed to have developed a weak urge to lean against him for support.

Sternly, Kay fought against it. 'I was just wondering if that cluster of roses looked too heavy on this side of the bower.' She rushed into hasty speech to cover her confusion. 'Do you think I've put in too many? Or not enough?'

Her voice dropped away into an abyss of silence.

York considered the bower for an endless, stretched minute. 'It looks fine to me,' he said at last, and something told Kay he was no longer looking at the roses.

Perhaps it was the deep undertone of his voice, so close to her ear, that told her his head was bent downwards over her own, instead of looking up at the bower.

Perhaps it was the sensation of something drifting ghostlike across the silky sheen of her hair, so lightly that it could only be his breath, and even that made every hair on her head tingle from its root to its very tip.

She thought, 'If I'm not careful, it'll come out spiky in the morning.'

'I want to go and get cleaned up. I'm tired, and grubby.' She meant her excuse to sound brisk, firm and matter-of-fact. It came out sounding more like a plea to him to let her go, and she could have kicked herself as she felt the vibration of his silent laugh against her back.

The pressure on her hair became firm and unmistakable, and it was not York's breath that caused it now. Kay went deathly still. 'I came to bring you in to supper,' York said.

'Is that the time?' Kay pretended surprise. It was not very convincing, since the dusk in the marquee was already slipping over the edge of darkness. 'I don't think I'll bother with supper,' she hedged desperately. 'I'm not hungry.'

There was a strange, aching hunger inside her, but it was not for food, and she refused to let herself contemplate what might satisfy it. She rushed on, hardly aware of what she was saying, urgent only to break the unnerving contact with York that was doing sensational things to her metabolism. 'You'll want to be alone with your family. You'll want to talk.'

'You're my guest, Katie.' With firm hands he turned her round to face him. 'I don't starve my guests. Not even ones as stubborn as you. So come and get your wash, and join us in the drawing-room for a drink and some sandwiches before you go to bed.'

And, bending his head, he sealed his command with a light brush of his lips across her mouth, that set it throbbing all the way back to the house.

It gave Kay a strange feeling to know that she would be York's guest for only one more night. The job for which she had come to Canon Court was done. Tomorrow, the chefs and the waitresses would take over, and apart from some last-minute supervision, she herself would become just another guest. And after the ball in the evening was over, like the others, she would go home.

And that would be that. Life would return to normal.

But not quite normal. Subtly, life had changed since the day she had met Louise in Wychwood. It had changed even more since she came to stay at Canon Court. Was it only a few days ago? It seemed more like a lifetime.

She herself had changed.

'Living here has given me a taste for the high life,' she told herself derisively, and thrust her forebodings to one side. She would forget her stay at Canon Court as easily as one forgot a summer holiday the moment the cases were unpacked, and life resumed its old routine.

It might not be so easy to forget York.

The uneasy thought pursued her, and to escape it she flung herself into the last hectic preparations on the wedding morning. The staff arrived early, and Kay closeted herself in the kitchen with the head chef for as long as possible. He soon took over with professional competence, leaving Kay free to her own devices.

It was too early yet for her to change into her own outfit and, feeling rather forlorn, she left the kitchen—where she had reigned supreme for the last week—in the charge of the head chef, knowing how Bess must have felt when she herself took over.

Eveybody else in the house seemed to be fully occupied, and with nothing left for her to do until she went to the church along with the other guests, Kay felt distinctly *de trop*.

She had seen York only once that morning, hurrying about some errand or other, and she caught her second glimpse of him now, coming in her direction, his arms loaded with bouquets from the hothouses for Louise and her two bridesmaids.

Kay deliberately turned away in the opposite direction, and York called out to her, 'There's a box of buttonholes on the hall table. Choose whichever one you'd like, to go with the colour of your outfit.'

Without waiting to hear her mechanical, 'Thank you,' he hurried upstairs with the flowers, to where Bess and Louise were closeted with the bridesmaids in the lengthy process of dressing themselves in their finery.

Kay did not feel entitled to butt in on the gathering, for fear she might offend Bess. Feeling rather like the proverbial waif in the storm of busy occupation going on round her, she chose a yellow carnation, and retired to the window-seat in the drawing-room.

She was sitting down somewhat dispiritedly, when she saw that the bridegroom had chosen the same refuge as herself.

'I could do with a strong cup of coffee,' Dave groaned, looking so abject that Kay was surprised into a laugh.

'You've just given me a job,' she chuckled. 'In fact, I'll make a pot of coffee, and bring some cups on a trolley in case someone else feels the need of a strengthener as well.'

They were sitting sipping their drink together when York and Oliver Tait ran them to earth ten minutes later.

'Kay! It's great to see you again.' Her ex-boss grabbed her and kissed her heartily on both cheeks, and Kay laughed at his exuberance.

'It's good to see *you*. How are you?'

'Fit as a flea,' Oliver grinned, and then sobered. 'Though I'm in the most ghastly jam at the moment. I've had to impose on York to help me out of it.'

'Have a cup of coffee, and tell me.'

Kay poured two cups, carefully avoiding York's eyes as she gave one to him. 'Guest trouble?' she hazarded, thankfully turning back to the distraction of Oliver.

'Worse,' he grimaced. 'Gas trouble. There's a suspected leak along the street somewhere near to the Melton, and all the nearby buildings have had to be evacuated until it's found, and dealt with.'

'Evacuated?' Kay's expression reflected the hotelier's dismay. The Melton was Oliver's premier hotel in that part of London, and would be crammed with summer visitors to the capital at this time of the year. Added to which, Oliver lived in the penthouse there himself.

'What on earth are you going to do with the guests?' Kay cried. 'For that matter, what are you going to do yourself?

There won't be a spare room of that calibre to be found in
London at this time of the year.'

Oliver frowned. 'I'm not bothered about myself. But I
lived on the telephone all day yesterday. Slotting in the
guests wherever I could. Most of them have gone to the
other hotels in the chain.'

'Have you got them all settled now?'

'All except six, and I've left my secretary frantically
trying to find rooms for them. As it happens, they're all
wedding guests here, but unfortunately they've come from
overseas, and they're combining the wedding with a
sightseeing holiday. They're booked in at the Melton for the
next three weeks,' he groaned, 'which is why I've come on
my bended knees to ask York to take them in.'

He turned to his host. 'When I left, Shirley still hadn't
managed to find suitable accommodation, so it looks as if
I'll have to take advantage of you, old man. Naturally, I'll
supply the staff. I wouldn't expect your housekeeper to cope
with such an influx, and I'll pay you any sum you like to
name if you'll only give them a roof over their heads until
the gas leak's been dealt with. Even the marquee would do,
at a pinch.'

His tone was jocular, but there was no doubting the
seriousness of his predicament. The kind of people who
booked in at the Melton would expect their path to be
smoothed at every corner, no matter what the difficulties
encountered by the hotelier, and in a way, they were York's
responsibility too, since they were wedding guests, even
although he might not know them personally.

Kay looked across at York. Why did he not say yes, right
away? she wondered, surprised by his continuing silence. It
would not put him to much trouble, to help Oliver over his
difficulty. Canon Court could swallow a small army of
guests, without even noticing. Her ex-boss was beginning to
look puzzled, too, as well he might, Kay thought
indignantly.

York continued to look thoughtful. 'Did you mean what
you said, about being willing to pay any sum I like to
name?' he asked slowly, and Kay stared.

Was York mercenary, as well as unfeeling?

Surely he would not have the nerve to charge his friend? she thought incredulously. Oliver could well afford to pay anything he might ask, however outrageous. Although the hotelier chose to live simply, he was an extremely wealthy man. But so was York.

'Of course I did. Name the damages,' the latter urged. 'They'll be high.'

'The cost to the Melton's reputation will be higher still, if I can't house my guests in suitable accommodation.'

'In that case,' York said quietly, 'I take it you'll be prepared to help finance a therapeutic pool at our local cottage hospital?'

Finance a therapeutic pool! It was the stuff of her own and Helen's dreams ever since they had come to the cottage, and Kay wondered if her ears were deceiving her.

Oliver had no such reservations.

'You're on,' he said promptly, 'although naturally I shan't want my name linked with the reason for my interest.'

'Naturally,' York agreed gravely, and as if in a dream Kay watched the two men shake hands on the deal.

Oliver would want the extent of his involvement to remain under wraps anyhow, Kay knew. She was one of the very few poeple who knew of his frequent and generous charitable gifts. But what was York's motivation? Was it purely for Sam's sake. Or was he doing it to impress Helen?

If it was the latter, Kay realised uneasily that even when she left Canon Court, she was unlikely to have seen the last of York. If Helen was the reason, he would still be a frequent visitor to the cottage.

Through a daze she heard Oliver say relievedly, 'I'll have their luggage brought along, and I'll draft in some staff to help cope in the house.'

'Hold on a minute,' York admonished him. 'Don't be in such a hurry.'

What was coming now? Kay wondered bewilderdly. The arrangement was cut and dried so far as she could see.

'I'll put you up, of course, Oliver,' York said easily. 'But as to your six guests . . .' His look swivelled to encompass Kay, and she had a sudden, unnerving feeling that he was about to spring a trap on her. 'It all depends upon Kay,' he said.

'On me? Why me?'

'If I'm to entertain house guests, I must have a hostess.'

'They won't need entertaining,' Oliver protested. 'After the wedding, they intended to sightsee in London. I can arrange for a minibus to take them into town each morning after breakfast, so you needn't be bothered by them at all.'

'I couldn't possibly abandon them altogether,' York put in. 'They're Louise's wedding guests, after all.'

Kay drew in a hard breath. York could conveniently remember that, when it suited his own purpose, to tighten the screw on herself.

'They'll be here for dinner each evening. No, I insist,' he declared, as Oliver made to speak. 'They'd expect to go back to the Melton for dinner as a matter of course, so they must feel free to do the same in their temporary quarters here. Which is why I must have a hostess. And a cook, of course.'

He gave Kay a look that dared her to accept his challenge. And dared her to refuse it, knowing what the outcome could mean for Sam.

'I couldn't possibly,' Kay blurted. York had manoeuvred her into his trap with malicious cunning, and she searched her mind wildly for a way out.

'I'll reimburse you. And I'm sure you're quite capable.'

Kay had often acted as Oliver's hostess when he had business entertaining to do. But to act in a similar position for York? No, she could not, would not, agree to such a preposterous suggestion.

It would mean she would have to remain at Canon Court, and to accept the position of its unwilling chatelaine. A spurious position, at York's side, that was wholly repugnant to her.

Also, it would be for an indefinite period of time, for who knew how long it would take to discover and fix the gas leak? Was York so immersed in his own selfish world that he did not remember she and Helen had a business to run, on which their living depended?

'It's out of the question,' Kay declared. 'I must go back home. Helen can't possibly cope with all our party bookings single-handed, and we can't let our regular customers down.'

York gave her a long, considering look that made Kay suddenly want to curl up inside herself. 'Without Kay's help, I'm afraid the answer has to be no, Oliver,' he said.

'I could lend your sister a chef for however long it takes, Kay,' Oliver offered. 'One of the men who's here today would stay on, I'm sure.'

Kay bit her lip indecisively. The two men waited. Oliver's eyes pleaded with her, and she found she could not meet them. The hotelier had unhesitatingly come to her rescue when she needed help herself. How could she refuse him now?

And there was Sam. His small, limping figure hop-skipped across her mind, accusing her. Just as York knew it would, she thought furiously.

Yet to give in to York's outrageous demand upon her time, without at least a token resistance, stuck in her throat.

'I'll have to ask Helen,' she prevaricated.

'Ask her now. Here she is,' York said, and made Kay's bewilderment complete as her sister and Sam walked into the drawing-room to join them.

'Ask me what?' Helen enquired, and Kay answered in a strangled voice, 'York will explain.'

She herself felt incapable of doing so. She felt as if the control of her own life was slipping out of her grasp, and she listened with resisting ears as York put Helen in the picture, and then with growing dismay as her sister applauded the plan.

'That's marvellous!' Helen exclaimed. 'Marvellously generous of you, Oliver,' she praised the hotelier warmly as they were introduced, and turned with shining eyes to Kay. 'Just think what a pool at the cottage hospital will mean, Kay,' she cried. 'It's what we've dreamed of!'

So why should the realisation prove to be such a nightmare? Kay asked herself savagely, as she slipped into her simple silk suit, multi-patterned in greens and yellow, and pinned the yellow carnation on her shoulder.

'How did you get here? Did you manage to coax Sam to travel?' The two questions spilled out as she walked with Helen and Sam and the other guests the short journey across the park to the estate Church.

Helen looked surprised at her ignorance. 'No, of course not. We came by pony and trap. York sent the groom for us this morning. Didn't he tell you?' As Kay shook her head, 'I expect he meant it to be a surprise. I think York thought you might feel a bit left out of things, with all Dave's relations and friends, and their own, and no one you really know except himself and Louise. And Oliver, of course. It's a pity York doesn't follow his sister's example,' she added mischievously. 'He's got a beautiful home. It's just crying out to be filled with children.'

Kay cast her sister a startled look as they filed into their pew in the tiny estate church, and the service began. York looked tall and distinguished, carrying out his duties of giving away the bride with complete aplomb.

She tried to imagine him standing a little further to the right, in the place of the bridegroom. Who, she wondered idly, would then be standing in the place of the bride? Did Helen see herself in that role?

The thought popped ready-made into Kay's mind, and gave her such a jolt that she almost dropped her prayer-book. She made a desperate grab to save it, and Oliver looked round from where he stood beside Helen, carefully holding Sam standing on his chair so that the child should be able to see what was going on.

'Are you all right, Kay?'

'Yes, fine. Just clumsy, that's all.'

Kay managed to retrieve the errant volume just in time, and ducked her head over it, hiding her face as she feverishly searched for the lost page.

What on earth had put such a fantastic idea into her head?

But was it so fantastic? She knitted her brows, remembering Helen's own words. 'I like him a lot. In fact, I could fall for him myself.'

What if her sister had not been teasing? What if she really meant what she said? Helen made no secret of the fact that she enjoyed York's visits to the cottage, and it might not be simply for Sam's sake that she welcomed him.

Once the idea entered Kay's mind, it persisted like an irritating mosquito, and she was still mentally swatting at it when Louise walked back along the aisle, radiant on Dave's arm.

Kay found her own reaction as disquieting as the idea that provoked it. She expected—nay, hoped—that Helen would one day get married again. So why should she feel so disturbed at the thought that York might be courting her sister?

Kay dismissed her thoughts impatiently. The prospect of York as a brother-in-law was enough to disturb anyone.

She followed the others out into the sunshine, and watched as the photographer posed and clicked, and when he had finished, she shook rose petals over the happy couple, along with all the other guests, as bride and groom climbed into their open carriage for their triumphal return to the marquee and the reception.

The head chef and his staff had been busy during their absence. The buffet table looked positively baronial, as Kay had intended it should, and the wedding cake was resplendent upon its own separate table.

Many were the admiring comments Kay overheard among the other guests as she made her way towards the bower she had erected for Louise and her bridegroom, and she felt an unexpected lump rise in her throat as her friend kissed her warmly, and said, in a little catching voice that was quite unlike the normally self-assured air hostess she knew, 'Thanks for everything, Kay. It's out of this world. You've been an absolute angel.'

And then another guest took her place, commanding the bride's attention, and Kay passed on. A hovering waitress handed her a glass, and she took it absently and drank, gasping as the wine stung quick tears to her eyes that she was positive had not been lurking there before.

After her own lucky escape from Mervyn, she was the last person to shed sentimental tears over someone else's wedding.

'Feeling sorry for them, Katie? Or are you feeling envious?'

It was York. What evil luck had made him bump into her, just as she was dabbing her smarting eyes, confident that she was well hidden among the crush of people in the marquee?

Kay spun round, to the imminent peril of the wine in her glass, which rocked alarmingly up to its rim.

'I don't feel anything, one way or the other,' she snapped. 'I'm a hard-boiled career girl. Or hadn't you noticed?'

'Maybe I'm a mite unobservant,' he drawled.

He was not. His eyes took in every detail of her flushed cheeks, of the wildly shaking wine that the almost-full glass must have told him was not the cause.

'Drink it, before you spill it,' he advised her, and added as she automatically began to raise the glass to her lips, 'Stay here. I'll bring you some food, and we can eat together.'

Kay did not want any food. Particularly, she did not want to eat it with York. If she swallowed turkey, she would be sick, and the last thing she felt inclined to do was to put up with York's derision if she refused to eat it.

The only thing to do was to make good her escape before he came back. Kay gave a hunted look round her, and discovered to her dismay that she was completely hemmed in by chattering guests.

Disregarding the danger to her wine, Kay turned and tried to push her way through the crush, but her slight figure was unequal to the pressure of smartly dressed bodies, and before she had managed to make the slightest impression on the wall of humanity surrounding her York was back, and holding two filled plates in his hands.

People made way for him, Kay saw crossly, and gave a stricken look at the plate he held out towards her.

Look what we've got for you:

5 FREE GIFTS

. . . A FREE compact manicure set
. . . plus a sampler set of 4 terrific Harlequin Romance® novels, specially selected by our editors.

FREE MYSTERY GIFT

. . . PLUS a surprise mystery gift that will delight you.

All this just for trying our Reader Service!

With your trial, you'll get SNEAK PREVIEWS to 8 new Harlequin Romance® novels a month—before they're available in stores—with 11% off retail on any books you keep (just $1.99 each)—and FREE home delivery besides.

Plus There's More!

You'll also get our newsletter, packed with news of your favorite authors and upcoming books—FREE! And as a valued reader, we'll be sending you additional free gifts from time to time—as a token of our appreciation.

THERE IS NO CATCH. You're not required to buy a single book, ever. You may cancel Reader Service privileges anytime, if you want. The free gifts are yours anyway. It's a super sweet deal if ever there was one. Try us and see!

Get 4 FREE full-length Harlequin Romance® novels.

Plus this handy compact manicure set

Plus a surprise free gift

▼ PLUS LOTS MORE! MAIL THIS CARD TODAY ▼

Harlequin's Best-Ever "Get Acquainted" Offer

Yes, I'll try the Harlequin Reader Service under the terms outlined on the opposite page. Send me 4 free Harlequin Romance® novels, a free compact manicure set and a free mystery gift.

118 CIH FAUN

PLACE STICKER FOR 6 FREE GIFTS HERE

NAME _____

ADDRESS _____ APT. _____

CITY _____

STATE _____ ZIP CODE _____

Gift offer limited to new subscribers, one per household. Terms and prices subject to change.

PRINTED IN U.S.A.

Don't forget...

...Return this card today to receive your 4 free books, free compact manicure set and free mystery gift.

...You will receive books before they're available in stores and at a discount off retail prices.

...No obligation. Keep only the books you want, cancel anytime.

If offer card is missing, write to: Harlequin Reader Service,
901 Fuhrmann Blvd., P.O. Box 1867, Buffalo, NY 14269-1867

BUSINESS REPLY CARD

First Class   Permit No. 717   Buffalo, NY

Postage will be paid by addressee

Harlequin Reader Service ®
901 Fuhrmann Blvd.
P.O. Box 1867
Buffalo, NY 14240-9952

No Postage
Necessary
if Mailed
In The
United States

'I didn't bring you any turkey.' He caught her look, lips twitching, and Kay's eyes flew to his face, unable to decide whether to feel grateful for his consideration, or to hurl her plateful of alternative food at his taunting grin.

A large woman in an enormous cartwheel hat turned to speak to York at that moment, and under cover of its umbrella-like proportions, Kay managed to dodge round its owner, and thread her way with what speed she could muster out of the marquee, and on to the blessed spaciousness of the lawn.

Glen ambled across the grass to meet her from where he had been lying sprawled beside the house doorway, obviously waiting for his master to emerge from the scrum, and impulsively Kay presented her plate to the surprised Rottweiler, and had great satisfaction in watching its contents disappear into the dog's grateful jaws.

Reluctantly she returned to the marquee in time to join in the champagne toast, and receive her allotted piece of wedding cake. Shortly afterwards Louise and Dave left to catch their plane.

The inevitable anticlimax set in when the bride and groom were gone, and people began to drift towards their cars to go to home or hotel room, to change ready for the ball in the evening. The bustle meant Kay had no opportunity to speak to Helen in private, and she waved away her sister and Sam as the pony and trap set off, and blinked at the prick of tears that were dismayingly real this time. She should have been going home with them. Kay watched the trap disappear round a bend in the long drive, with a disquieting feeling that when eventually she did return home, things would never be quite the same again.

Black depression descended upon her as she made her way back to the house, wondering what arrangements, if any, York expected her to make for his unexpected guests. Oliver had lost no time, she noticed. Two Tait Hotel vans, in their familiar maroon-and-gold livery, were already at the door unloading suitcases. She would have to hurry.

The moment she got inside the house, she sought out one of the regular day staff, who were doing extra duty today because of the wedding.

'The rooms are all ready, Miss Courtney,' the woman assured her. 'When Mr Tait phoned Mr York first thing this morning, we opened up the west wing just in case he couldn't manage to get his guests booked in anywhere suitable. They're in their rooms now, and they seem to have settled down happily enough.'

First thing this morning . . .

So York had known about Oliver's difficulty hours ago, and had tentatively agreed to the arrangement long before he blackmailed Kay into being his hostess. Unscrupulously, he had used the crisis to his own advantage to interfere yet again in her private life, and keep her away from the cottage.

There could be only one reason why he wanted her to do that. He was holding her hostage to give himself free access to the cottage, and Helen!

'He shan't get away with it,' Kay vowed. 'I'll have it out with him the minute I go downstairs.'

Her dress gave her confidence. She needed to look her best in order to do battle with York. She wore no jewellery, relying for effect on the subtle beauty of the muted jade silk, shot through with delicate gold embroidery. The high, sleeveless bodice was softly pleated, and the skirt opened out in a wide fan from Kay's tiny waist. A glance in her mirror gave her all the confidence she needed to confront York. Clutching her gold evening bag, she hurried downstairs.

The impromptu house party gathered in the drawing-room foiled her intention from the start. The moment she appeared through the doorway, York beckoned her to his side, and began to introduce her to the guests.

Oliver was there as well, which helped, and fortunately Kay had no need to murmur more than a few conventional politenesses. The two senior guests took charge of the conversation. They were elderly, American, and vocally delighted at their good fortune in finding themselves housed in a genuine, lived-in, 'olde ancestral home'.

They were typically charming and friendly, and they did

not care if the gas leak kept them away from the Melton for the rest of their stay in England. Uncharitably, Kay prayed their dream would not be realised.

The other guests proved to be a honeymoon couple, who Kay suspected would not have cared if they had landed in the middle of a desert island, and a young, engaged pair, who shared their views.

Not a very demanding house party. Certainly not one that needed the services of a hostess to keep them happy. York could very well have coped on his own if he had wanted to. But of course, he did not want to, for very good reasons of his own.

Kay attached herself ostentatiously to Oliver when the time came for them to repair to the ballroom, but once inside the doorway York took the initiative again. Cutting across Oliver's invitation, 'Shall we . . .?' he reached out and drew Kay to his side, and held her there with her hand tucked under his arm, as he began to greet his arriving guests.

Kay was too startled by his unexpected move to be able to circumvent it, and she stood there stiffly, fuming in silence as people began to file past them. She had agreed to play hostess to York's house guests, but to deliberately place her by his side in the ballroom was to infer a very different kind of relationship between them altogether.

York introduced her to each person in turn, safe in the knowledge that she could not rebel in front of strangers, and Kay's anger against him mounted as the trickle of people became a persistent queue, and the ballroom steadily filled.

He offered no explanation of Kay's presence with him, not even to those people he seemed to know well, and Kay herself was obliged to remain silent in respect to Oliver's wish. Her fury knew no bounds as she read the open conjecture in the passing faces.

By now, the whole ballroom was probably buzzing with rumour as to what she was doing there, and she cringed at the direction which some of that rumour might be taking. At the moment, she felt she could have cheerfully slain

York for putting her into such an invidious position.

She shook hands mechanically and smiled until her face felt stiff, but when the last guest had arrived and she thought her ordeal was over, York drew her masterfully into his arms, and swung her on to the dance floor to open the ball with him, thereby mutely confirming what many of the guests must be thinking, to judge by their sly glances at her ringless left hand.

'What did you drag me into doing this for?' she demanded in furious undertones as they circled the floor.

'Because you're acting as my hostess. And it's a hostess's duty to greet her guests.'

'They're not my guests. They're yours. I only agreed to act as hostess to your house party. Goodness knows what these other people must be thinking, having me welcome them here tonight as if . . . as if . . .'

She floundered to a halt, her cheeks firing.

'As if what, Katie?' York mocked, and the glint in his eyes dared her to finished her sentence.

The words stuck in Kay's throat. He did not need to ask. He already knew what she meant. And he was deliberately goading her, knowing that she couldn't create a scene in front of a ballroom full of people.

Kay's glare was vitriolic as she met the laughter brimming in the black eyes looking down into her face.

Laughing, because he knew, and could not care less, what his guests might be thinking.

As if he found the direction of their thoughts highly amusing.

CHAPTER FIVE

AFTER the opening dance, to Kay's relief, York left her in order to circulate among his guests.

She did not lack partners, but she quickly discovered that her ordeal was far from over. Without exception, before they had completed a circuit of the room, each new partner managed somehow to bring up the subject of her presence at Canon Court.

One or two questioned her openly. 'Is there an engagement in the offing?' Turning their question into a joke to excuse their curiosity.

Others went about it more adroitly, but in whichever guise the question was put, it all added up to one thing. They wanted to know what was Kay's position at Canon Court, and in particular what was her relationship with York?

The middle-aged ones were the worst, she discovered. Their interest was no doubt heightened by their natural concern for their own daughters. York was an eligible catch, with his background of wealth and breeding, to say nothing of his lovely old home. Kay hid her scorn with difficulty, masking her anger behind a brittle smile, and giving to each one the same brief answer. No, there was no engagement in the offing. She was acting as hostess to help a client out of a difficulty.

After which she pointedly changed the subject, blocking the way to further questions, which the thinly disguised doubt in her listeners' faces told her would otherwise continue indefinitely.

She felt livid with York for subjecting her to such an inquisition. She doubted if anyone present would have the temerity to question him personally, which left her to bear the brunt of the situation which he had deliberately created.

After the umpteenth question-and-answer sparring match, Kay's patience was stretched to breaking-point, and she was just about to quit the ballroom no matter what impression her absence might give, rather than endure another moment of the third degree, when Oliver came to claim her next dance.

'I'm endlessly grateful to you, Kay, for helping me out,' he told her warmly as he waltzed her round the floor, and made Kay instantly ashamed of her rebellion.

'Forget it,' she answered. 'Think how the pool will benefit Sam.'

'He's a great little fellow, isn't he?' Oliver smiled, and his voice was wistful. 'Tina and I would have loved children of our own. Even one would have been a help, now.'

A child would have given the hotelier someone to live for. In spite of everything, Helen was lucky to have Sam, Kay reflected, but all she said was, 'Getting the pool project off the ground will keep you on your toes. Helen's over the moon about it.'

'I'm going to the cottage to see her tomorrow. She's agreed to steer me through the local contacts. Sam's consultant at the cottage hospital will be the first one. We'll need his backing to get the plans passed.'

Typically, once he embarked on a course of action, Oliver did not waste any time. It was the same dynamism that had built his hotel chain into a universal symbol of success, and with his driving power behind the scheme, Sam's pathetic paintings of imaginary swimming pools should soon be turned into reality.

Remembering it helped to get Kay through the rest of the evening, during which she managed to avoid York until the MC announced the last waltz.

York literally took her out of the arms of her last partner, so that Kay had no opportunity to escape him, although she objected strenuously as he waltzed her away.

'You ought to have the last waltz with one of your guests. The American lady . . .'

'I mustn't single out one of my guests. It might make the others jealous.'

'How typically conceited of you.'

York grinned. 'Isn't it?' he agreed, and swung her into the dance.

The music was a langourous lilt, and because it was a bride's ball, the tunes the orchestra played were all suitably dreamy and romantic, making Kay wish irritably that she had hired a steel band instead.

But the subtle beat of the music had an insidious effect upon her, however much she tried to steel herself against it. The haunting quality of the notes was mesmeric, drawing the claws of her anger, and unconsciously Kay began to relax, and respond to the fluid grace of York's steps.

Unlike her other partners he danced in silence, which made a refreshing change, and if she had been dancing with anyone else she might have been able to forget whose arms they were that held her, and given herself over completely to the enjoyment of the dance.

With York as her partner, that was impossible.

He guided her expertly, steering clear of collisions with other couples in spite of the crowded room, and then the lights overhead went dim, and there was only herself and York enclosed in a small private bubble of darkness, blown along on the whispered breeze of the music.

The darkness was no defence against him.

If anything, it served to increase Kay's awareness of the man whose arms wrapped her in bands of steel, completing an electric circuit that sent shock waves of sensation pulsing through her veins as they danced.

It must be tiredness that was allowing York to get through her guard like this, Kay excused the inexplicable frailty of the guard she had so successfully erected round herself since Mervyn.'

Desperately, she tried to strengthen her armour by making believe that she was dancing with her ex-fiancé, but when she closed her eyes to heighten the illusion, she discovered to her consternation that she could not recall a single one of Mervyn's features, and only the dark, hawklike face of her partner floated under her closed lids, as if it was printed indelibly on her inner vision.

She opened her eyes again quickly, but the picture refused to go away, even though she pressed her forehead against York's jacket to try to get rid of it, refusing to look up at his face and turn the illusion into reality.

The pressure on his jacket front was the merest touch, but he was alert to her every movement, and responded instantly by tightening his hold upon her, and moulding her slight figure even closer against him. The move brought into sharper focus the feel of his hand on her back, warm against her skin through the delicate material of her dress. His other hand, firm and strong, closed masterfully round her fingers. His was a vital, male attraction that would not be ignored. Tiny electric currents probed at her nerve-endings, rousing a stirring excitement inside Kay that not all her self-discipline was able to subdue.

With mounting frustration, she knew from the increased pressure of his hold upon her that her responses were getting through to York loud and clear.

Bewilderment added to Kay's tension. Hating York, she despised herself for feeling his attraction, which was purely physical, she told herself firmly. Weddings traditionally left the guests, as well as the bride, dewy-eyed, and in spite of her claim to be immune, the atmosphere must have got through to her. It made her feel as if she was two selves in one, each warring with the other, and she longed to wrench herself free from York's arms, grab up her belongings, and flee back to the cottage, her family and safety.

Yet even there she would not be safe from York, because he would make the swimming pool the perfect excuse to continue coming, in order to see Helen.

The lights went up again as suddenly as they had dimmed. They brought the world back, and Kay blinked herself back to normality as the tempo of the music increased to a quickstep.

The tune changed to Auld Lang Syne, and then there was a bustle of people collecting wraps, and exchanging goodbyes, and York moved among the waiting cars outside, a tall, elegant black-and-white figure, speeding his departing guests.

If only she could have been among them!

Now the day was finally ended, Kay felt fit to drop. All that she wanted to do was to roll into bed, pull the covers over her head, and sleep the clock round. And forget York, and all the complications he was raising in her life.

But as his hostess, her day was not yet ended. There were still the six guests to be attended to, seven if she counted Oliver. Kay turned and made her way wearily towards the drawing-room, hoping against hope that they all felt as tired as she did herself, and had already made their various ways to bed.

She opened the door, and discovered the guests clustered round a tray of fresh coffee and sandwiches, resurrecting the events of the day as enthusiastically as if they had only just got up.

Kay groaned inwardly, and helped herself to a coffee, leaving it black in an endeavour to prevent her eyelids from closing completely. If only York would come, and speed these last of his guests off to bed!

A puff of air from the door opening behind her whispered the folds of her skirt about her feet, and her wish was answered. Even through her weariness, Kay knew it was York, and not Oliver.

Fingers of ice crackled down her spine, registering his approach from behind her, and her tiredness took on a new dimension, and became merely a background exhaustion that still left her nervily alert to his every movement as he came unseen towards her across the deep pile of the carpet.

He reached her side, and from what seemed a long way away, Kay heard a cheerful American voice enquire, 'Do you have any ghosts running about here, Mr Demster? Your house is sure old enough to be haunted.'

'Only this one,' York said, and his fingers came under Kay's chin, and tipped her face up to meet his keen look.

'You're as white as any ghost,' he chided her, ignoring Kay's fiery blush that set his words at nought and then immediately receded and made them true again, only leaving her face this time even whiter than it was before.

'Bed,' York commanded her.

'No, I'm . . .'

Kay could cheerfully have slain him.

What on earth had possessed her to wish he would come and join them? How dared he order her to bed, as if she was two years old, and in front of guests to whom she was supposed to act as his hostess? Kay squirmed with

embarrassment under his hold, but his fingers were
remorseless, gripping her chin in a vice she could not break
free from without an undignified struggle.

'You've been on your feet since six o'clock this morning.'

So had he. Earlier, in fact, Kay knew.

'You'll have an early start tomorrow. I'm sure our guests
will excuse you now. It's been a long day for you.'

It seemed still longer before he let go of her chin.

Kay's eyes sparked defiance, but she knew it was
pointless. The guests were all murmuring their agreement
with York, no doubt silently commending his consideration
for her, when Kay knew that it was only in his own interests
he was doing this, to make sure she was up in time to cook
their breakfasts the next morning. Humiliated and angry,
she had no option but to answer their smiling goodnights,
and do as she was told. Do as York had told her to.

She flashed him a vitriolic look as she put down her
coffee cup, and pinned a smile on her face for the benefit of
the guests. *Our* guests, York had called them. As if she was
a permanent resident at Canon Court.

She had not danced with any of the three male guests
during the course of the evening, so they had not been in
receipt of her own standard explanation of her presence
here.

If they heard it now, she realised, it might embarrass
them, since they were bound to feel themselves the cause of
putting their host to extra trouble and expense on their
behalf.

What, if any, explanation had York given to them? Or,
arrogantly, had he chosen to give them none at all, being a
law unto himself? The latter was the more likely, and Kay
was scowling as she nodded goodnight to Oliver as she
crossed the hall.

The hotelier made for the drawing-room, and as he
opened the door she heard York say, 'You're the last one in,
Oliver. I can lock up now.'

York came out of the still-opened door, and Kay felt his
glance shaft upwards, following her as she mounted the
stairs, but resolutely she steeled herself not to look back.
She continued climbing, her back rigid, resisting his stare,

and then his footsteps walked on across the long hall, releasing her as he made his way to slide the bolts on the thick oak door.

Kay had almost reached the landing when a sudden question flashed across her mind.

She had to obtain an answer to it now, right away, before the guests dispersed for the night. It would be too late in the morning. If she was quick, she could slip back into the drawing-room while York was checking the front windows, and be back and up the stairs again, unnoticed, before he returned.

Picking up her long skirts, Kay turned and ran lightly downstairs, and sped back to the drawing-room.

She was on her way out again, her information gained, when York returned, much more quickly than she had expected him to, and caught up with her as she reached the foot of the stairs.

She backed defensively against the newel post as he stopped to face her.

'Were you looking for me?'

'No.'

'What brought you back to the drawing-room?' One eyebrow arched in satirical enquiry. 'Don't tell me you wanted a drink of water?'

'I forgot something.'

Kay leaned back against the hard wood of the newel post, and her lips set in a mutinous line.

First, she had had to endure inquisitions from York's guests. And now, from York himself. He was treating her like a child, demanding to know why she had come downstairs again, after he had sent her off to bed.

'You had your bag in your hand when you went upstairs, so why . . .?'

Kay's eyes flashed angrily. She refused to give him a detailed explanation of her every move. Because he had blackmailed her into staying on at Canon Court, it did not give him the right to dictate her every waking moment.

'Why I came back downstairs is nothing to do with you.'

His eyes narrowed at her defiance. 'Everything that goes on under my roof is to do with me.' He moved closer to her, looming over her, suddenly menacing, and Kay shrank closer to the newel post, her heart beginning to beat uncomfortably fast.

'There's nothing going on, as you call it. I told you, I'd forgotten something.'

'I wonder what it was you forgot?'

His eyes were mere slits of darkness in the shadows of the hall, and impulsively Kay turned to run up the stairs away from him, but quick as a flash his hands went out, pressing on to the newel post on either side of her, imprisoning her.

He held her there without touching her, and she had no room to move unless it was to turn into his arms. If she did that, they might close round her, and she desisted hastily.

She shrank from having York touch her again. She felt too tired. Too vulnerable.

'Was it this you forgot, Katie?'

York bent his head. Kay's eyes widened into a startled vision of black hair, black brows, and gleaming black eyes closing in on her, and then all detail merged into a blur as his lips closed over her mouth, and all the crazy, mixed-up sensations she had managed to subdue since the last waltz, surged into tingling life again inside her.

'Is that what you came back for, Katie?'

'I ... it ... oh, for goodness' sake, let me go!' She wrenched her head free. 'They'll be coming out of the drawing-room any minute now. They'll see ...'

The mocking tilt to York's lips said he did not care, and Kay cast a desperate look towards the drawing-room door. They were coming out now. She saw the knob start to turn, and a transatlantic voice boomed through the growing slit, 'Well, I guess I'm too tired to stop up and watch for any ghosts haunting the corridors tonight.'

'Let me go,' Kay whispered frantically.

'Tell me what you came downstairs for?'

'Oh, you ...' His arms hemmed her in, as immovable as the newel post that was making carved patterns into the soft flesh of her shoulders. The drawing-room door opened wider, letting light spill out.

Kay's breath hissed through her clenched teeth. 'If you

must know, I came down to find out if any of the guests were vegetarian.'

'Are they?'

'No!'

The explosive monosyllable unlocked York's hands from the newel post at her back, and his arms dropped to his sides.

'Goodnight, Katie. Sleep tight.'

His lips brushed lightly across her forehead, and Kay jerked her head away and fled up the stairs, followed by his low, mocking laugh.

She slowed down, panting, when she reached the landing, and her eyes winged down. York was still there, his one hand resting negligently on the top of the newel post, his one foot on the first stair, silently watching her panic-stricken retreat.

People grouped out of the drawing-room, and York turned away to bid his guests goodnight, and Kay flung into her room and began to tug at the zip of her dress with fingers that shook so much she had difficulty in retaining hold of the slender catch.

In spite of her tiredness, her sleep proved far from restful. York's dark, sardonic face haunted her dreams as effectively as any ghost, and she sat up in bed with a gasp as a sharp knocking sound penetrated the wraiths of rousing consciousness.

'Good morning, Miss Courtney.' A neat chambermaid, whom she recognised as being one of Oliver's loan staff, approached her bed bearing an inviting-looking tray of tea things. 'I was given instructions to call you at seven.' The girl smiled, and put the tray down on Kay's bedside table.

Bless Oliver! He knew she must want to sleep the clock round, and he had chosen this method of making her early rising as painless as possible. Kay sipped at the hot tea gratefully, and in little over half an hour she was showered and dressed, and making her way downstairs to the kitchen, to tackle the breakfast chores in readiness for half-past eight.

Faint smudges of shadow still lurked like tell-tale bruises under her eyes, betraying the nervous tension of the last twenty-four hours, but the familiar environs of the kitchen calmed Kay as she searched out fruit, cereal packets and eggs, and started on the routine task of preparing the meal. She was half-way through arranging segments of grapefruit in cool blue and white porcelain bowls when York stuck his head round the kitchen door, and sniffed appreciatively.

'That coffee smells good. Is there a cup going?'

Without waiting for Kay to answer, he helped himself to one of the cups standing ready on a tray, and began to pour from the percolator.

'Do you *have* to?' Kay shot him an exasperated look. 'I'd put those cups all ready for the breakfast-room.'

She grabbed another cup and saucer out of its cupboard, and clattered it into the gap on the tray, ostentatiously glancing at her watch as she topped up the depleted percolator.

'There's plenty of time. It isn't eight o'clock yet.' York propped himself easily against the nearest worktop, and proceeded to watch Kay while he sipped his coffee.

'No, there isn't. The guests are booked to spend the day at Windsor, and I've promised to provide a hamper for them to take along.'

With York standing so close, watching her at work, Kay's fingers felt all thumbs, and she wished crossly he would go away. The knife she was using with such ease before he came slipped, and with a sharp exclamation she snatched her finger away in the nick of time.

'Can't you take your coffee, and drink it somewhere else?' she snapped.

'Why? Do you need something from out of this cupboard?'

He did not move an inch from his lazy stance against the cupboard doors.

'No. I . . . you . . .' Kay groped for words.

'Does me being here put you off your stroke?' he wanted to know amusedly.

'No' would be a lie, and York knew it.

If she said 'yes' it would be an admission of just how easily he managed to get under her skin.

Kay glowered at him.

'Can I join you? I'm dying for a coffee. It's all that booze you tanked us up with yesterday, York.' Oliver breezed into the kitchen, and saved Kay from having to reply, and hurriedly she bent to extract another cup and saucer from its shelf, thankful for the opportunity to hide her face.

On second thoughts, she added another cup and saucer to the first. She felt in need of a strong coffee herself, and not because of any surfeit of wine the day before.

Except for a flush that could easily be caused by bending down, Kay had her expression under control again and she rose from the cupboard and, handing Oliver his filled cup, she said gratefully; 'Thanks for the tea first thing. It was a life saver.'

'Not guilty,' the hotelier disclaimed. 'It must have been York.' And, carrying his cup, he began to circle the kitchen, interestedly assessing its facilities.

'Guilty,' York drawled, and his look lanced through Kay.

She bent her eyes hastily to the grapefruit, rattling the bowls together on to a tray in an alarming castanet that threatened their survival.

'Thank you,' she managed in a muffled voice.

The fact that York had sent her the tea tray caught her off-guard, and while he stood watching her, waiting for her reaction, she felt unable to cope with the discovery, or with the irrational warmth that spread through her because York had performed the small act of kindness, and not Oliver.

The silence in the kitchen stretched endlessly. Oliver was still absorbed in cookers and deep freezes, and Kay cast about urgently in her mind for something to do. The fruit was finished. The guests could help themselves to cereal if they wanted it. It was too early yet to begin cooking eggs and bacon. If she picked up her coffee cup, she would have to look up from the worktop, and she knew if she did, she would not be able to avoid looking across at York. His eyes drew her with a hypnotic pull that she found almost impossible to resist.

'The guests are all down now, Miss Courtney. Shall I sound the gong for you?' One of the two waitresses loaned by Oliver had come briskly into the kitchen, and Kay spun to greet her with effusive relief.

'No, you carry in the coffee and the first course. I'll sound the gong.'

Kay ejected through the door as if it was an escape hatch, and expended her pent-up nerves on the gong. She felt a lot better as she made her way back to the kitchen, and her cooling coffee.

One glance round the room told her that she could enjoy her drink in peace. York and Oliver were both gone, presumably to the breakfast-room in obedience to her noisy summons.

Left to her own devices, Kay made short work of cooking the breakfasts, and with the two waitresses to do the fetching, carrying and subsequent washing up, she was able to concentrate on filling a good-sized hamper for the six guests, before sitting down to enjoy her own brief repast.

Oliver came in to collect the completed hamper and stow it in the minibus, waving away his excited guests en route for Windsor with their chauffeur, who was also to act as their courier for the day.

The hotelier had planned to go and see Helen this morning, to set in motion the plan for the swimming pool, Kay remembered.

'I'll go with him,' she decided aloud. After a week incarcerated at Canon Court, the house felt like a prison, and it would be a refreshing change to escape back to the cottage, if only for a few hours.

Lunch was to be a cold collation, so she had the rest of the morning free, and it would only take minutes to load the sideboard when she returned. Dinner was not until half-past seven, so she did not need to commence cooking until mid-afternoon.

'Go with whom, where?' York enquired from the doorway.

Kay spun round from the peg where she was hanging her overall, and eyed him balefully.

'With Oliver, to the cottage,' she clipped. After her experience in the hall last night, she knew better than to refuse to answer him. 'Oliver's going to see Helen this morning about the swimming pool.'

'You're a mite late to catch up with him.'

'He can't be gone already. He's only just seen the minibus away.'

'After which he jumped straight into his car, and by now he'll be half-way down the drive.' York peered out of the window. 'If you don't believe me, come and look.'

Kay believed him, but she looked just the same, in time to see the tail-light of the Jaguar disappear round the bend in the drive.

Her face registered her chagrin, which quickly turned to anger as she met the, 'I told you so,' glint in York's eyes.

'I'll take our van and follow him,' she declared, determined not to be denied her outing.

'You're too late for that, as well. Your van's not here.'

'Nonsense. I left it parked by the side of the house. Helen didn't go home in it. She can't drive. And anyway, your groom took her and Sam back in the trap.'

'It's because Helen can't drive that your van's parked in the garage at the cottage right now.'

'You're talking in riddles,' Kay snapped, feeling her temper rise.

York explained with exaggerated patience, 'It was no use Oliver lending Helen a chef in your absence, if the man isn't able to deliver the orders. To do that, he had to have your van. Oliver arranged for the chef to put up at your local pub so that he's handy to the cottage, and he took the van with him when he finished up here last night.'

'How did he get hold of the keys?'

'You gave them to me yesterday, to put the van inside for you, because a delivery lorry was blocking the way. Remember?'

Kay remembered, and her temper spilled over.

'You'd got no right to give him the keys without asking me first. It's my van!'

How dared he dispose of her property, as well as her time? Outrage choked her utterance.

York shrugged. 'It's Helen's van, as well as yours. She agreed to the chef taking the vehicle.'

'Neither of you bothered to let me know what you'd

done, or to ask me if I minded.' If she wanted evidence that
York was driving a wedge between herself and Helen, this
was it. 'Thanks to your interference, I'm marooned here
until further notice,' she realised furiously.

'If you want to go out anywhere, all you have to do is to
ask me.'

'Ask your permission, I suppose you mean? Please, sir,
may I, sir? No thanks,' Kay spat.

'In that case, since you don't appear to want my services
as a chauffuer at the moment . . .'

'I do *not*.'

'I'll go on my rounds of the farms, and leave you in
peace.'

Pieces would be a more adequate description of the way
she felt at the moment, Kay thought bitterly. York seemed
to be completely unmoved by their encounter. He strode out
of the kitchen on his way to his accustomed Sunday
morning round of the farms, and left Kay shaking with a
mixture of anger and frustration, and something else which
was difficult to define, but which held a disturbing hint of
fear in it.

Fear that York's arrival in their lives would succeed in
destroying everything that she and Helen had managed to
build up together?

York's own life had not changed one whit, Kay thought
resentfully. He had succeeded in turning her plans upside-
down to suit his own convenience, but he was serenely
doing his rounds of the estate exactly the same as usual. In
fact, he was carrying on his own life unchanged, completely
uncaring for the turmoil he was causing in hers.

Kay took her troubled thoughts out on to the terrace, in
the hope that the bright morning sunshine would blow
them away. She considered walking across the park to the
church, and then remembered that the local vicar ran two
parishes, and was ministering to his other parish in the
morning. The other parish church was all of six miles away,
and she no longer had the van.

The morning dragged endlessly. The newspapers were
obsessed with political news, and Kay thrust them aside in
disgust. For once, walking did not entice her. A dragging

weariness from the day before dissuaded her from exercise, and she flung herself moodily on to a long lounger, yearning for distraction from her own unwelcome thoughts. She wondered listlessly how far York had got on his rounds of the estate. Was he sitting comfortably in the farmhouse even now, with his own mid-morning refreshment taken from the brown crock teapot on the stove in Mrs Jim's capacious kitchen? Perhaps he was playing with the puppy, if it had not already gone to another home?

If it had, Kay wondered if the little creature was feeling as bewildered as she was herself. Still, if the pup was already with another owner, it would solve the problem of York trying to foist the animal on Sam.

Kay wondered wearily if he would continue his visits to the cottage, now the wedding was over. If he did, it would prove his interest in Helen.

She would have to wait until the afternoon for her question to be answered, and, to rid herself of the tension of uncertainty, Kay took her tray back to the kitchen and started to prepare the cold buffet for lunch.

However dedicated the chef, there was a limit to the amount of time that can be spent fussing over salad and cold meats, and there was little left for her to do afterwards, except to drag out the time by changing her clothes ready for lunch.

Her pale violet dress was unremarkable on its hanger, but the stark simplicity of the cut flattered Kay's perfect figure in a way that made embellishments unnecessary. She chose a delicately chased brooch of Mexican silver to go with it, and a matching silver bracelet, and with those clipped into place she still had half an hour left before she needed to go downstairs again.

She leaned her arms on the window-sill, and brooded at the view. She was not watching out for York's return. Perish the thought! But disliking their owner did not prevent her from enjoying the view of the broad acres of his estate.

She would miss them, she realised suddenly. The comparatively restricted view from the cottage windows would seem positively claustrophobic when she returned. It must be pleasant to wander in the woods in the cool of the evening, and bring back handfuls of dainty bluebells for the vases, she thought, her mind wandering so that she did not notice the distant speck on the park road grow steadily larger until the smooth purr of an engine alerted her to the return of the Range Rover.

She remained where she was, at the window. York would go on along the tarmac strip to the front of the house. But instead of continuing past, the Range Rover pulled to a halt at the barred gate leading on to an inner road through the gardens. He must be going to garage the vehicle in the stable block at the back of the house, as was his wont if he was finished with it for the day. Did that mean that he intended to remain at home for the rest of the afternoon?

How easily the word 'home' tripped through her mind, Kay thought with a sense of shock.

She watched him speculatively as he slid out of the driving seat, and approached the gate. As he reached out to pull back the stout bolt, he looked up, straight at the house.

Hastily, Kay backed away from the window, and knew from the quick tilt of York's head in her direction that he must have seen her.

If she had remained still, he might not have noticed she was there at all, but it was too late now to do anything about it. She felt oddly breathless, as if she had been running, and furious with herself for idling at the window in the first place. York was bound to come to the one conclusion that she would have done anything to avoid. She had *not* been watching out for his return. But inevitably, his overwhelming conceit would assure him that she had.

His greeting, when she went reluctantly downstairs a little while later, told her that her guess was right on target.

'Did you miss me, Katie?' he greeted her as she walked into the dining-room.

'I hadn't even noticed you were gone.'

She turned her back on him, and dallied at the sideboard, helping herself to far more food than she wanted in an effort to cool her burning cheeks before she faced him again.

'You should have come along with me.'

'Nice of you to offer, now it's too late.'

'You said you didn't want my services as a chauffeur.'

Trust York to turn her own words against her! Kay bit into a celery stick with a crunch that satisfied her sudden need to destroy something.

'Phew, what a morning! I've trekked miles, and talked to dozens of people. I'm immersed in swimming baths up to here.' Oliver burst into the dining-room, clutching his forehead in mock exhaustion.

'Sorry I'm late for lunch, folks,' he apologised. 'Helen wanted me to stay and have it at the cottage, but I simply must go to town this afternoon to see how they're getting on with that gas leak, and if I'd had lunch with Helen and Sam I'd have been tempted to stay on, and let the Melton get along without me.'

Oliver's bubbling enthusiasm about the swimming baths project kept the conversation flowing, and usefully masked Kay's preoccupation until the hotelier hurried back to his Jaguar with the promise, 'I'll be back at the same time as the guests, Kay.'

What time would York be back? Or would he not be going at all?

The clip-clop of hooves sounded from the gravel, answering her, and York said, 'I must be off, too, or Sam will think I'm not coming.'

Kay was about to open her mouth to speak, when he answered her other question, unasked.

'I won't need a picnic hamper. I told the chef to put in a nice selection of untouched dishes from the kitchen into the van, when he took it last night, and to let Helen have them, to save her the bother of cooking for herself and Sam today.' He smiled. 'When she rang last night, she said the chef had brought enough to keep them for a week, so she'd provide the picnic from that.'

York's words removed any doubt in Kay's mind that York was interested in Helen. And that her sister must be equally interested in York. She had rung the Court last night and spoken to York, but not to herself.

A feeling that she tried not to think was jealousy flashed

through Kay. And disconcertingly, a question tracked unheralded across her mind. Was it jealousy of York? Or of Helen?

To confuse her still further, another question presented itself, and York answered that one unasked, too.

He seemed as if he could read her mind as clearly as a computer screen, Kay thought irritably, and vowed to guard what she was thinking in future when he was around.

'It's a pity you can't come to the cottage as well,' he remarked, with no real sign of regret. 'But with dinner to cook for this evening . . .'

He had not the slightest intention of inviting her along, and by depriving her of the van he had made doubly certain that she could not go independently. A mixture of anger, disappointment and resentment warred inside Kay in a bitter conflict. York had gone out of his way to save Helen from having to cook for herself and Sam, but he showed no compunction at all in expecting her, Kay, to cook for an entire house party.

His airy wave as he sent the pony trotting briskly away from the house showed that he didn't mind in the least that he was leaving Kay behind.

She turned away and attacked the preparations for dinner, dicing and chopping with a ferocity that threatened the safety of her fingers but, in spite of her efforts to keep her thoughts from straying, her concentration wandered. No matter how she tried to stop it, her mind insisted upon following York. Thanks to him, it seemed a lifetime since she had enjoyed a peaceful Sunday afternoon in the company of her family.

What were they doing now?

The kitchen clock told her they would have already reached the riverbank. Kay had seen the obligatory fishing-nets propped up in the front of the trap when York left, waving derisory flags at her as she watched the con-veyance disappear along the drive.

Was Sam already fishing? Perhaps leaning out over the shallow water, intent upon his weekly treat of hunting for minnows, with the sturdy black dog dutifully on guard beside him, in case he leaned over too far?

It struck Kay unexpectedly that, in spite of her protestations to the contrary, she had enjoyed the carefree picnics.

The realisation took her by surprise, and her knife stilled. She, too, had enjoyed the picnics!

It was only because of the fun Sam derived from them, of course. But without York, and his pony and trap, Sam would not have been able to enjoy them at all.

Even if she and Helen had been able to take Sam as far as the river on their own, if York had not been there, would the picnics have been such fun without him?

Kay shied away from her own question, and continued slowly with the preparation of the dinner. She felt slightly light-headed, as if she was standing outside of herself, and watching something burrow to the surface through the sternly resisting dam of her subconsciousness.

And knew a terrible dread that if whatever it was managed to break through, it might split the barrier wide open, and release a flood that would drown her.

Oliver and the guests arrived back just before seven o'clock, and by half-past they were assembled in the dining-room, where Kay joined them as the waitresses began to serve.

York had not returned, so in his absence Oliver took his place at the head of the table, with Kay in her usual place at the foot. To her relief, she had little need to talk. The guests came in bursting to relate the events of their day, and any gaps in the conversation were usefully filled in by Oliver's progress report on the gas leak.

No, it had not yet been traced, so he must beg their indulgence for a little while longer.

Unanimously the guests made it flatteringly plain that they considered they were the ones who were being indulged, but so far as Kay was concerned, their compliments fell on deaf ears.

Why had York not returned from the cottage?

She picked at her own dinner without appetite. He had not telephoned. Did that mean he had started out from the cottage, and had some mishap on the way? Had the pony bolted, or . . .?

Common sense routed her momentary panic on that score. The steel strength encased in York's wrists was more than enough to prevent a pony of that size from bolting. Which left only one alternative.

York must be still at the cottage. And he hadn't telephoned because he didn't want to.

Surreptitiously, Kay glanced at her watch. It was gone eight o'clock. Sam would be in bed by now. And York would be with Helen, alone together in the quiet parlour downstairs.

Was he kissing Helen, the same as he had kissed herself?

Kay's dessert-spoon dropped with a clatter, and bounced from the table to the floor, creating a confusion that was no match for the confusion of thought that exploded like a meteorite shower inside her head.

Hating York, for a brief, dreadful second, she found herself hating Helen, too.

Kay bent hurriedly to retrieve her spoon from the floor, miserably aware that even the act of ducking her head below the level of her knees could not bring back the colour to her bloodless cheeks.

She used the excuse to push away the rest of her sweet uneaten, and sat tensely toying with her wineglass, hardly conscious of the conversations going on round her. The words bounced against Kay's mind like so many raindrops battering at a window-pane, running away, not penetrating. She felt physically sick. And all because York had not arrived back for dinner.

His absence was neither here nor there, she told herself, since the guests were primarily Oliver's responsibility, and the hotelier slipped easily into the role of host, rendering York's presence unnecessary. It was not as if he had left her to do the entertaining on her own.

So, what on earth was the matter with her? Why was she so concerned by York's absence?

'You're quiet tonight, Kay,' Oliver remarked, coming up to her as she dispensed coffee afterwards in the drawing-room.

'I'm still jet-lagged after yesterday,' she parried, and escaped to the voluble enthusiasm of the American couple before the hotelier could question her further.

One half of her mind registered their confession, 'Your country's great, but I must say hubby misses his steak for breakfast,' while the other half chewed unceasingly on York's continued absence like a tongue-tip probing the ache of a hollow tooth, although when Oliver himself voiced the question that occupied her mind, Kay shrugged it off lightly.

'Oh, I expect he's stayed on at the cottage, to help eat up the left-overs.' And laughed, and passed on to speak to someone else, as if it was a matter of the utmost indifference to her what York did or did not do.

And wondered why it should suddenly seem important, and could find no adequate answer to that question, either.

Kay contemplated telephoning Helen to see if York had actually left the cottage. But the possibility that he might not have done so, and—she caught her breath—of what situation her phone call might disturb, killed the idea almost before it had time to take root.

Kay threw herself into her duties as hostess with a verve that won her acclaim from the guests, and a probing look from Oliver as he watched her display of brittle cheerfulness which might deceive the guests, but did nothing to deceive Kay herself, or the hotelier, she suspected uneasily. It seemed to Kay's stretched nerves as if the evening would never end, but even the longest hours run their course, and she reached the blessed solitude of her room at last with a sigh of relief. Instinctively her feet carried her straight to the window, but since she had not bothered to switch on the light, she was not afraid of being seen, and the cool night air and the silence acted as a balm to her jangled nerves.

The wind was rising, as if it might portend a storm after the warmth of the day, and sounds reached her ears out of the night that had been masked by the noisy bustle of daytime activity. Small stirrings made by the old house as it responded to the cooling temperature, and stretched its ancient timbers, as old buildings will. A high-pitched yip-yip as a screech owl hunted its supper, and soft rustlings, as potential suppers crouched closer for protection against the ivy-covered walls.

Kay's ears took and sifted the sounds, and discarded each one, because none approximated to the clip-clop of a pony's hooves. Impatiently she pulled the window to, drew the curtains half over it, and made ready for bed.

She did not switch on the light, relying on the faint illumination of the moon filtering through the narrow crack between the velvets as she slipped out of her clothes, and into the demure cotton nightdress that made her look ridiculously young, with its dainty embroidered neckline, and wide, lace-edged frill reaching to just above her instep.

Although she pulled the covers right over her head, and tried to switch herself off and woo sleep, her ears remained alert for every sound coming from outside, and one day dissolved into another before sheer weariness finally released her into a restless doze.

She awoke she knew not how long later, with a feeling that she had forgotten something.

She racked her brain for what it could be, and frowned her puzzlement into the darkness.

Her wakened mind went back over the events of the evening, searching for an answer. Oliver had given his progress report on the gas leak. She had listened to the saga of the day's visit to Windsor, and the much-appreciated picnic hamper.

Kay smiled. At least the Americans had enjoyed the picnic, even if they considered English breakfasts fell short of their own at home.

That was it! She sat up in bed. Steak for breakfast. She remembered promising the guest a large piece, grilled rare, especially to suit him.

And she had forgotten to take it out of the freezer in readiness.

If she left it until the next morning, she would be faced with rock-solid steak, and a sadly disappointed American.

Kay peered at her bedside clock. Two-thirty. If she went downstairs now, and took the meat out of the freezer, there would be plenty of time for it to thaw out before morning. She need not bother to tidy herself. No one would be there to see her.

Pushing her hair back from her eyes, she slid her feet out

of bed and wriggled them into her mules, and wondered if York had returned home in the meantime. Her dozing had been so light that she would surely have heard the pony's hooves on the gravel, if he had?

With herself safely imprisoned at Canon Court, there would be no one to question him remaining at the cottage overnight, if Helen wanted it that way, too.

A cold chill crept through Kay, and although she pulled her soft cashmere dressing-gown round her, its icy fingers followed her as she padded her way downstairs. She pushed open the kitchen door, and blinked at the bright light that met her.

York straightened up from the freezer.

'Well, well,' he drawled, looking her up and down. 'I thought for a minute we really had acquired a ghost, after all.'

CHAPTER SIX

KAY stared at York speechlessly.

'Did you think I was a burglar, Katie?'

Kay did not know what she thought. Her mind was only capable of grasping one thing. York had not stayed the night at the cottage. She felt a dizzy sense of relief that was as strong as it was puzzling.

'I thought . . .'

She stopped. York's look penetrated her mind, forbidding her to go on, and Kay's fingers clenched convulsively as his black eyes kindled. He knew exactly what it was she had been thinking, and his tilting brows mocked her thoughts as unworthy.

Dull colour stained Kay's throat, running up into her cheeks and forehead in a blaze of fiery guilt. She felt a defensive urge to burst out, 'If you haven't been at the cottage, where have you been?'

The question lay unspoken and unanswered, loading the air between them, as with an immense effort she managed to get her tongue under control in time, and altered the words to a stiff, 'Did you want something from the freezer?'

It was a silly question to ask. If York did not want something, he would not have the freezer door open.

'I was getting out a pack of my emergency rations.' York pointed a packet of fish fingers at her like an accusation. 'Care to join me?'

'Fish fingers?' Kay grimaced. 'No thanks. And there's no need for you to eat them, either. I kept your dinner for you. It'll only take a minute to reheat it in the microwave.'

When she had plated the meal and put it to one side, she had jeered at herself for doing something so utterly pointless. Now, she felt overwhelmingly glad that she had. The surprise on York's face more than compensated her for the slight trouble.

124

'To quote our American friends, that was "real dandy of you".' He slid the offending packet back into the freezer, but in the act of closing the door he paused. 'Now you know why I'm raiding the kitchen at this unearthly hour, what about you? What brings you ghosting through the house? You should be safely tucked up in bed.'

For a second time he questioned her reason for coming downstairs again, but Kay scarcely noticed. Overriding any resentment she had felt before at his questioning, was a curious kind of excitement. It welled up inside her, the same kind of catchy excitement she used to feel as she prepared for forbidden midnight feasts in the dormitory, only different.

Her mind jinked away from the difference.

'Steak,' she answered him briefly.

'Steak? After eating one of your own dinners?'

'It isn't for me. It's for the American guest. He likes it for breakfast.'

'Barbaric.'

'Not more so than our own grilled kidneys and bacon.' Kay advanced towards the freezer.

'Which cabinet?'

'The one you've got open.'

She wished it had been the other one, further away from York. Now she was over the initial shock of finding him in the kitchen, she was becoming acutely conscious of her own sleep-tousled hair, and unconventional dress.

York still held the freezer door open, waiting for her, and she had no option but to go forward to it. To him. She knelt quickly to the cabinet, and the sudden move finally unloosed the already slack knot of the belt of her dressing-gown, which abandoned its role, allowing the soft cashmere to part, and flower-sprigged cotton to spill out from underneath.

Kay's cheeks took on the same rosy hue of her dressing-gown, and her elbows went quickly to her sides to prevent its folds from slipping any further. She could not send her hands to the rescue, because they were full of steak, and York was already closing the door of the freezer. His eyes fired, laughing at her discomfiture, and Kay searched frantically for the nearest flat surface on which she could deposit her burden, and leave her hands free to grip the loose, warm folds round her again.

'Allow me.' Instead of taking the steak from her, York left her hands manacled to the icy package, and took hold of the errant dressing-gown instead.

He took his time pulling it round her, allowing his eyes to wander from her scarlet cheeks across the low-scooped neckline of her night-dress, down to her two rows of small toes peeping through the fluff of her mules, each one feeling as hot as her cheeks with embarrassment.

'You're lovely, Katie,' he murmured.

His hands burned hot fire through the folds of her dressing-gown, and a strange expression fleeted through his eyes, making them impossible to meet. The excitement built up inside Kay to fever pitch, accelerating her pulse to a breathtaking speed that made the blood thump in her ears.

Over the pounding, York's voice sounded oddly hoarse. 'You're lovely, Katie . . .'

He stopped, and with an abruptness that was almost brutal he tugged the fronts of her dressing-gown together, took hold of the belt, and knotted it with a force that made her gasp in protest.

'Too tight?' He loosed it to comfort pitch. 'Where do you want the steak left?'

Now he took the package from her, grabbing it out of her hands and pivoting away without waiting for her answer.

He would have to wait a long time. Kay swallowed with a throat that felt suddenly parched. Wordlessly she indicated a worktop, and York deposited the steak. Still keeping the table between himself and Kay, he said curtly, 'Where did you put my dinner?'

'I'll get it for you.'

She did not doubt that York was capable of getting it himself, and manipulating the microwave oven, but she urgently needed something to occupy her hands.

'While you do that, I'll make us some coffee.'

It sounded as if he intended her to share some part of his gone-midnight feast, but the excitement had vanished. Perhaps it was only in her own imagination that it had been there at all?

York poured himself a cup of coffee without waiting for it to finish perking, and gulped it black while he waited for the rest to finish. As if he needed it urgently, Kay thought dully, and told herself, 'He must be hungry. He can't have had anything to eat since the picnic this afternoon.'

Where he had been since then was his own business. 'It doesn't concern you,' she insisted silently, and wondered why her mind had to repeat even more firmly, 'it *mustn't* concern you.'

She fished out a tray cloth, and placed knife, fork and spoon in position, working automatically, aware all the while of York behind her, bending to the cupboard to get out cups and saucers. Aware of the clink as he placed one on the other, and added spoons to each. Tiny, everyday sounds, elevated to sharp significance by her heightened senses.

York poured a cup of coffee out for Kay and another for himself, placed a chair for her at the table, and sat down opposite to begin on his delayed meal, with the width of the wood between them.

When he finally pushed away the empty plate, he looked up and across at Kay, and said, 'Thanks, Katie. I needed that.'

'It's your own fault you didn't have it at the proper time.'

Kay bit her lip vexedly. She had not intended to comment on York's absence from the evening meal. She determined to ignore it altogether, as being too insignificant to mention, but the words slipped out before she could stop them, and she could feel his eyes follow her as she took the plate to the sink, and let it drop on to the stainless steel top with more force than she intended, to cover her slip.

'I wouldn't call a bull calf exactly my fault,' York responded drily as she returned with the afters and without thinking cut a slice of lemon meringue and slid it on to a plate, the same as she would have done for the family if she had been at home.

'I'm sorry. I should have left you to help yourself. I wasn't thinking.'

'That'll do fine for me.' York accepted the plate and continued, 'The animal chose the darnedest time to arrive in the world. But considering his mum's my showpiece, and it's her first calf . . .' He dug his spoon into the sweet, and for the first time Kay noticed the deep lines of weariness drawing his face. 'I hope the guests understood the urgency, when you explained why I couldn't make it for dinner tonight?'

'How could I explain? I didn't know myself.'

York's head jerked up. 'The stockman phoned you.'

'No one phoned me,' Kay denied flatly, trying, and failing, to keep the ire out of her voice.

York frowned. 'I told him to contact you, when he went to ring for the vet. I wish now I'd asked Helen to ring you instead. By the way,' he digressed, 'talking of Helen——' They were not. They were talking of why York had opted out of the evening meal without having the courtesy to let Kay know, but she let it pass, and he went on, '—Sam sent a picture he painted for you, I left it in the Land Rover. I'll put it in the kitchen for you, first thing in the morning.'

'Helen knew where you'd gone?'

'Yes. The stockman got in touch with me at the cottage, because I'd left instructions that I wanted to be there when Sheba calved. But I reckoned I'd be back easily in time for dinner, and I said if I couldn't make it, I'd ring you from the farm.'

'It must have slipped the stockman's mind.'

'He'd got a lot of things on his mind at the time. He had trouble in getting hold of the vet. He had to put through a number of calls before he finally made contact, because the vet was out. And afterwards, I gave him umpteen jobs to do at once. When I knew I might be late, I asked him to stable and feed the pony, and put out the Land Rover, ready for me to come back home in.'

So that was why she had not heard the pony's hooves returning, Kay realised, as York continued, 'By the time the man got back to the calving pen, everything was happening at once, and I didn't have time to check to see if he had managed to get through to you. I just took it for granted that he had.'

As he took a good many things for granted, where she was concerned, Kay thought.

'It wasn't important,' she answered, and knew it to be a lie.

And knew, too, as she left York to go on his nightly locking-up rounds—mounting the stairs with his, 'Thanks for the meal, Katie,' ringing in her ears and the light brush of his lips burning a track of fire across her forehead—that the thing which was burrowing its way to freedom inside her was very close to the surface.

Sam's painting was propped up on the worktop when Kay descended to the kitchen the next morning. She took it to the window with her coffee, and nearly dropped the cup in surprise when she looked at it.

Expecting to see the familiar picture of a public swimming baths, her startled eyes encountered splodges of black and brown and green, instead of the usual all-pervading blue.

Kay stared at the paper, puzzled. There were some odd-looking spikes, in pairs, but what . . .?

She turned the picture the other way round, and the spikes revealed themselves as ears. One pair graced a pony, and the other pair, a dog. The painting was a remarkably lifelike rendering of Sam's view from where he habitually stood between York's knees in the front of the trap, going on their weekly jaunts.

No, this was coming back, Kay realised. Two jam jars, filled with identifiable pictures of minnows, hung on the trap brasses.

So far as Sam was concerned, York had almost performed his miracle. Kay's eyes blurred.

She ought to be feeling jubilant. Over the moon, for Sam's sake. So why did she feel this sick depression instead, warring with all sorts of other mixed-up emotions to which she could not give a name?

Kay wondered what Helen thought of the picture. Its

implications would be sufficient to tip the scales in York's favour, whatever he chose to ask of her sister. With the picture to add icing to the cake, Helen would be ready to lick York's boots if he asked her, Kay thought with a flash of anger. Although, from the amount of time they were spending in each other's company, he was more likely to ask Helen to marry him, and polish his own boots for the occasion!

Kay beat the breakfast steak with a savagery that shocked her, but the result was an instant success at the breakfast table. On the strength of it she ordered extravagantly for another delivery, and hoped York enjoyed steak too, because if the gas leak got mended today, he was going to have a lot left over in the freezer to eat up when she and all the guests left Canon Court.

The thought added to her depression, leaving her even more confused than before. Oliver sought her out after breakfast was over, and invited her, 'Come with us today, Kay. The guests all want to visit a real old English pub, so I'm taking them to the one in the village for lunch. After trekking all over Windsor yesterday, they don't feel like venturing far today, and the Royal Oak's got all the necessary ingredients, like oak beams and all that sort of thing, which should satisfy them. It'll save you from having to cook a midday meal, as well.'

Kay accepted with alacrity. 'I'd love to.'

Her depression lightened at the prospect, and she gave herself plenty of time to change into a neat green trouser-suit and matching slip-on shoes, suitable for the outing. She decided against taking a bag. Her suit had pockets which would hold her hanky, and anything else was unnecessary.

It was lovely to feel free, she thought light-heartedly, as she made her way downstairs.

Through the open front door she could see the waiting minibus, and York's Land Rover parked nearby. The guests were already forgathered, and Oliver was talking to York.

The latter was not coming with them. At breakfast-time, Kay had heard him say that he would be working as usual during the day, and the assurance added to her sense of freedom.

She paused as she reached the hall. They were not due to set off yet. She would have time to check in the kitchen, to see if all the gas taps were turned off before she left. She felt reluctant to bump into York this morning. By dinner that evening, when meeting York could no longer be avoided, Kay hoped the events of the day would have succeeded in restoring her sang-froid. Her encounter with York in the kitchen last night had left her feeling restless and uneasy, and even in the clear light of day, the shadows still trailed like mist wraiths in the recesses of her mind.

The sound of an engine cut through the morning silence, then receded, and Kay cocked her ear to listen until it faded away in the distance. That would be York, gone about his business for the morning.

She shut the kitchen door behind her, and made her way outside.

'Oliver?' She stared at the spot where the minibus had been, and now, was not. Oliver's car was gone as well, she saw.

'Oliver's gone,' York said, and unwrapped himself from the bonnet of the Land Rover. 'By the way, did you find Sam's picture? I left it for you in the kitchen.'

'Yes. Thank you.'

Kay compressed her lips. She refused to comment upon the picture. No doubt Helen had already told York what a huge step forward for Sam, the boy's painting revealed, and Kay had no intention of adding to the family's adulation. She glanced at her watch.

'I might as well wait here for Oliver to come back. He said they'd be setting off at half-past eleven, and it's gone a quarter-past now.'

'Oliver isn't coming back. The minibus is taking the guests on a sightseeing tour round the lanes, and Oliver's joining them at the pub at lunchtime.'

'But . . . he asked me to go with them . . .'

'I told the chauffuer not to wait. You're coming with me, instead.'

'You told him *what*?'

Disappointment turned to fury, and Kay rounded on York, her eyes flashing.

'Of all the insufferable, high-handed . . . you've got no right to change my arrangements!'

Kay's over-charged nerves exploded, and in a rush of pent-up feelings she stormed, 'How dare you interfere in what I'd planned to do?'

'Because I want to show you something . . .'

'I don't want to see it, whatever it is.'

'. . . at one of the farms . . .'

'I'm not going to one of the farms.' One visit to choose the turkeys had been more than enough for Kay.

'. . . and I've saved this morning on purpose . . .'

With unbelievable effrontery, York caught Kay up, and swung her into the high passenger seat of the Land Rover before she realised what he was going to do: and before she had time to gather her wits he climbed in beside her, and slammed the door.

'. . . so consider yourself privileged. I don't usually spend my Monday mornings showing people round.'

He had not listened to one word she had said.

Kay's temper erupted. With furious hands, she grabbed at the door handle, and pushed.

'Oh, Miss Courtney, I'm right glad you're going with Mr York.' Bess popped her head in through the opening, and beamed her satisfaction. 'I promised to send a cut-and-come-again cake for them to try at the Home Farm. It's a new recipe. It'll travel that much better in your lap than it would have done on the seat.'

The housekeeper reached up and deposited a large and heavy cake-box into Kay's surprised arms, and with a kindly nod said, 'Enjoy your visit,' and shut the Land Rover door again with a final-sounding slam.

'Enjoy your visit,' York mocked, and accelerated the vehicle away at a speed that made it impossible for Kay to jump out.

'I don't call it visiting, being dragged off against my will.'

'Tut tut, Katie. You make me sound like a pirate. A man's got a right to expect the company of his hostess.'

'You've got no rights whatever over me. I agreed to act as hostess to your guests. My place is with them, not with you. I'm not even employed by you, although you dispose of my time as if I was some kind of servant. I'm here at my own expense.'

She had emphatically rejected York's offer to reimburse her.

'Not quite at your own expense.' His voice was silky smooth.

'What else would you call it?'

'Call it a working holiday. After all, Oliver's paying a chef to take your place at the bakery, so you won't be out of pocket.'

Out of pocket she might not be, but out of countenance she certainly was. Infuriatingly, there was not a thing she could do about it, without breaking her word to Oliver.

Kay gritted her teeth. If it were not for the disastrous effect upon the steering, and the risk of a crash, she felt overwhelmingly tempted to end the life of Bess's good fruit cake across York's arrogant head.

Before she could succumb, the Land Rover drew to a halt by some farm buildings, and York opened the passenger door, removed the tin from Kay's hands, and gave it to a small boy who ran out to greet them.

'Take that into the house to your mother. And drop it at your peril,' he warned the laughing youngster, and turned to help Kay down from her seat as the boy ran off, and a man took his place who, from the likeness, Kay guessed was the child's father.

'How's everything this morning?' York asked him.

'Fine, Mr York. No problems.' He eyed Kay curiously, and York introduced them.

'This is Miss Courtney. Neil, my stockman. He's the culprit who forgot to ring you when I asked him to, last night.'

'I'm right sorry about that, Miss. I was in a fair old tizzy at the time, it being Sheba's first calf.'

'It wasn't important.' Kay forgave him, and the barbed look she shot at York said it was of supreme unimportance to her personally.

'Come and see the calf, miss,' the stockman invited proudly, and began to lead the way, but Kay hung back, and York sent her a hard look.

'There's nothing to be scared of. The calf won't bite.'

His contempt bit. It seared like acid, and Kay's voice sharpened to match. 'I don't want to see it.'

'You're just being stubborn, because I let the minibus go off without you.'

'No, I'm not. I . . .'

'What other reason can there be, except sheer contrariness?'

'If you must know, I don't want to see the calf, because I don't want to think of it as ending up as veal in another week or two,' Kay burst out, goaded by the pressure York was putting on her.

The episode of the turkeys had left an indelible impression upon her, and she did not think she had the courage to face another similar experience.

'I'll wait for you in the Land Rover,' she mumbled, and turned away.

York's hand shot out, detaining her. 'It won't be like that for the calf.'

His voice was unexpectedly gentle, and surprise turned Kay in her tracks to face him.

'I thought bull calves . . .?'

'This is a very special bull calf. He's the first from my champion, and the start of a brand new strain. The Canon strain. He'll be the most cosseted calf alive, and he'll live to a ripe old age, and sire generations of calves just like him.'

While he was talking, York was steering Kay firmly by her arm, step by step in the wake of the stockman. Just as he had steered Sam to the pony and trap, she remembered. Obliging her feet to walk alongside him, when their every instinct were to fly in the opposite direction.

Half of her longed to believe what York said, but the

other half was afraid to trust him, in case he was only saying it, in order to make her do what he wanted.

They walked across soft green turf to where a post-and-rail stockade held an open-sided shelter, providing welcome shade, and lined with a deep bed of sweet-smelling straw.

A cow nuzzled gently at a small form lying in the straw, but at their approach she looked round, and began to walk sedately towards the stockman stood at the rails. She stopped in front of him, and he reached out and fondled the big head, crooning soft endearments, and York grinned at the expression on Kay's face.

'He'd expire with embarrassment at the thought of speaking to his wife like that. Here comes the calf. He's nice and strong on his legs already.'

'He's a little beauty, guv'nor. He'll be a prize winner like his ma when he grows up.'

'Now do you believe me?' York slanted a look at Kay and his eyes held laughter, but the amusement in them was carefree, and not at her expense.

Unexpectedly Kay found herself laughing back as York said, 'If I dared so much as to mention veal in front of my stockman, I'd risk ending up on a chopping block myself.'

And he drew Kay forward to the stockade so that she could drop to her knees and put her hand through the rails to meet the small blunt muzzle, and feel the thrill of the hours-old calf rasping her skin with its rough little tongue, then beginning contentedly to suck her fingers.

The sun was warm on her back as she knelt, and from somewhere high above them the shrill, sweet notes of a meadow lark dropped like liquid gold on the scented breeze.

Kay thought suddenly, 'This is how is must have been in Eden.'

And sensed her hand reaching out beyond the noisy sucking of the calf, to touch some deep elemental need within herself, which she was at a loss to account for, but which she knew with a conviction that was stronger than reason, must somehow be satisfied, else it destroy her.

With her other hand she stroked the soft, golden coat, and York reached out to do the same, and their hands met on the little animal's back.

Kay's arm went rigid. Was it because she had stopped stroking, a second or two before York, that his hand had come to rest above her own? Under her palm Kay could feel the soft, silky warmth of the calf. Above it, she was agonisingly conscious of the firm strength of York's fingers, closing round her own.

Instead of moving on, and continuing to stroke the calf, they curled round her hand, sending a different kind of heat tingling through the delicate blue veins, setting her whole body alight, and making her heart thump madly in time to the paean of ecstasy from the lark.

Kay's breath caught in her throat. She couldn't look at York. Her neck felt stiff, the muscles knotted in a tight bundle of nerves between her shoulders.

From above her head Kay heard York say, 'I thought Sam might like to choose a name for the calf. It'll give him a sort of stake in it, and he'll enjoy watching it grow up.'

'He'd love that.'

Kay answered automatically. Her mind latched on to to York's words, 'he'll enjoy watching it grow up.'

It was a direct pointer to his own plans for himself and Helen, as well as for the calf.

The lark stopped singing, and an immense silence seemed to engulf Kay, trapping her in an empty, waiting void. Unrelated thoughts drifted in to fill it. All the confusing, jumbled-up thoughts that had so disturbed her mind for weeks, ever since she first met York.

But now they were no longer confused. They began to take on a coherent, recognisable form, and Kay watched the picture grow with a mixture of curiosity and dread. What were they about to reveal?

Unmistakably, they revealed her need.

Kay stirred, and her breath released itself in a long, shuddering sigh. Slowly, she turned to look at York, and her eyes held unquenchable anguish. They roved across his dark head, the familiar black brows that had frowned upon her so often. The lean, clean lines of his face, each one indelibly imprinted upon her mind.

Her need was York.

All her doubts and confusion were gone, vanished for ever in one terrible moment of self-revelation.

Her need was for York. And because of Helen, it must remain unfulfilled.

York was her Eden, and the unwitting serpent in the garden, was her own sister.

'Don't let the calf lick you any more. His tongue's rough. He'll make your hand sore.' Gently, careful not to hurt Kay or the calf, he pulled her hand away. He could be wonderfully gentle. She wished he was not. It undermined her defences against him, which she needed to strengthen more than ever now.

He raised her to her feet, and she allowed him to lift her without protest, too numb to feel any sense of soreness, except the immense, all-encompassing pain that locked her heart and mind in a shroud of ice, which she hoped desperately would never melt, because if it did, the agony would be more that she could bear.

Kay's mind was in a turmoil as she walked back across the paddock with York. She was barely conscious of putting one foot in front of the other. Only of the piercing pain of brushing against him as he stood aside for her to re-enter the door of the cowshed, and she obeyed woodenly, like a puppet, when he suggested, 'Come into the office before we start off again, and wash your hands where the calf's been licking you.'

The stainless steel wash-basin in a corner of the room gave her the excuse to turn her back for a moment, and she soaped and swilled vigorously, only vaguely surprised to find the water piping hot under the press-button soap dispenser, and disposable paper towels.

With her hands clean again, she protested, 'I could have washed when we got back home,' and winced at the deep well of longing the word uncorked, and threatened her self-control with a stream of hopeless tears.

'We won't be going straight home,' York answered. 'I

thought we'd carry on from here, and have a pub lunch, the same as the others.'

So York intended them to join Oliver and the guests after all. If only he had allowed her to go with them in the first place, how much misery it would have saved her.

But for how long? Kay wondered dully. How many days, or weeks, or months, could she have remained cocooned in her fool's paradise, before she had to come face to face with the truth of her love for York?

Her mind felt strangely detached, watching as she smiled and waved to the stockman with outward cheerfulness, as York helped her to clamber back into the trap, and took her with him to the front to sit beside him as he set the pony trotting back on the park road.

She was sitting in Sam's accustomed place, or nearly so. Not quite. Sam's place was standing between York's knees, with one of York's strong arms reassuringly round the boy.

Kay longed to feel York's arms round her, with a fierce, aching hunger that she must somehow find the strength to resist. York must not suspect how she felt. Added to her weight of misery, the humiliation of him knowing—at best pitying her and at worst jeering at her—would be too much.

Looked at logically, York and Helen would make an ideal couple. Sam worshipped York, so they would have no problems on that score. In fact, it was an ideal situation from every point of view except her own, Kay thought bleakly. She turned her head and gazed unseeingly at the passing carpet of bluebells, conscious only of the bell that tolled with leaden strokes inside her heart.

The pony stopped in the shade of a tree, and Kay blinked back to awareness of her surroundings. The pub was half timbered, magpie black and white, and a tourists' dream. But the hanging sign proclaimed it to be the Wheatsheaf.

'It's the Wheatsheaf,' she said.

'So it is.'

'But Oliver said he was taking the guests to The Royal Oak.'

'So he did.'

'Did he change his mind afterwards?'

'Not that I'm aware of.'

Kay's temper spilled over. 'Then what are you stopping here for? It's the wrong pub.'

She knew shock that it was possible to feel such anger against someone you loved so much that it lay like a deep pain inside. And that was another oddity, although after her experience with Mervyn, it should come as no surprise. Only the poets professed to believe that love made its victims happy.

York looped the pony's reins to a post, and gave it something from his pocket. 'We aren't obliged to stick with the guests. They're Oliver's responsibility during the day.'

He ducked under the low lintel, and steered Kay to a seat in a bow window, and ordered for her from a surprisingly generous range of dishes. When the food arrived, the aroma told Kay it was Italian cooking at its best.

The flavouring was subtle and delicate. The meat was a gourmet's delight. The vegetables were cooked to just the right degree of crispness. In fact, it was a dish Kay would have been delighted to cook, and eat, herself, but now she had no appetite for it.

'Don't you like it?'

'Yes. I'm just not hungry.'

She should have known that her efforts to eat would not deceive York.

'You just don't like admitting that anyone can cook better than you. If it was a dish from your own kitchen . . .'

York's taunt was the last straw. 'Thanks to you, it seems years since I cooked anything at all in our own kitchen.'

Her outburst was angry and bitter, vinegared with all the frustrations and misery that knowing York had brought in its train. She had to strike out at him or weep. So she struck, and knew from the tightness of his face that her aim was true. A small pulse ticked relentlessly at the point of his jaw.

'You haven't been away from the cottage for long. No longer than a normal holiday period.'

'It seems like a lifetime.'

Kay pulled no punches. So far as she was concerned, her stay at Canon Court was a disaster, and York might as well know it, although she would die rather than let him know the reason. Far from cementing their relationship, as Helen had so confidently predicted, it had left her with a legacy of unhappiness that would take years, if not for ever, to erase.

'I can't stay out all day,' Kay said petulantly. 'I've got the dinner to cook for nine people tonight, and it won't prepare itself.'

'You're wasting your time if they all peck at their food the same as you've done.'

'I told you, I'm not hungry.'

'Let's hope the guests will have better appetites. I'll give them something to help their dinner down, just in case. We'll open a bottle of champagne, to celebrate.'

'My cooking doesn't need anything to help it down! And anyhow, what is there to celebrate?'

Nothing, so far as Kay was concerned.

'There's the calf.'

The calf seemed a poor excuse to distribute champagne. Was York's desire to celebrate prompted by something—or someone—of even more importance to York than his cattle? What slight appetite Kay had had vanished altogether, and she gave up her pretence at eating, and pushed her plate away.

'Let's go back.'

York shrugged. 'Suits me.' Surprisingly, he didn't argue. In fact he didn't seem at all regretful about their early return, and his reason became apparent to Kay when he dropped her at the house door, and started off again with the pony and trap almost immediately.

To the cottage? It was a weekday, and Sam would be at school, so presumably he would find Helen on her own.

Kay attacked the dinner preparations savagely. So he thought her cooking needed something to help it down, did he? York's remark rankled, and although Kay knew she was deliberately blowing it up out of all proportion, fanning the flame of her anger against him because it helped to alleviate the pain she felt inside, she mixed ingredients with an extravagant hand that sent the calorie count of her dishes soaring, and would result in groaning bathroom scales the next morning.

She felt too miserable to care. Her head ached with a dull throb that made her doubt her ability to eat any dinner herself.

Towards the end of the afternoooon she heard the pony and trap return, but she ignored it, and continued to decorate pastries as if her life depended upon it.

'Those look smashing, Aunty Kay. Can I have one? I'm starving.'

'Sam! What brings you here?'

'Uncle York brought me.'

'Where's your mother?'

Kay's eyes flew over Sam's head to the door. York leaned negligently against the door post, but of Helen there was no sign, and the icing tube clattered from Kay's fingers on to the worktop, leaving a wildly uneven line down the length of the last pastry.

'Mummy's gone with Uncle Oliver to see someone about the swimming pool. She said to tell you she'd see you at dinnertime.'

'Dinnertime? Here? I don't understand.'

'That's right,' York nodded confirmation. 'So your efforts had better be *haute cuisine* tonight. There'll be a rival cook at the table.'

Helen was her rival in more ways than one, but that was a secret she must keep to herself. To ease the pang that shafted through her at his words, Kay snapped, 'I didn't notice you criticise what I served up to you last night,' and went suddenly pink.

For last night, read, the small hours of this morning . . .

Sam begged urgently, 'Can I have something, Aunty Kay? I'm starving.' His plea became a wail, and Kay grasped at the distraction gratefully.

'Have this pastry.' She slid it on to a plate, and gave it into Sam's eager hands. 'I spoiled the decoration on that one, anyway.'

'The icing's gone all wiggly.'

That was exactly how her stomach felt, and when Sam announced, 'Isn't it great? We're stopping here all tonight and all tomorrow night,' she asked faintly,

'Will someone please explain?'

'I just have,' Sam claimed indignantly.

'He just has,' York taunted, and Kay's lips compressed.
The glint in York's eyes said there was a lot of explaining to
do, and she would not enjoy the rest of what was to come.
Hurriedly, she turned back to Sam.

'Have you got permission to take time off from school?'

'I don't have to go to school. It's half-term.'

Kay had forgotten. In two short weeks, she was so out of
touch with events at the cottage, she had forgotten it was
half-term. And it was all York's fault. She rounded on the
author of her troubles.

'What about the bakery? The business won't run itself.'

'There's no need for you to worry about the bakery.
Helen's catered for everything, and she's left Oliver's chef
in charge. Now that Sam can travel again, even if it's only
for this short distance, it's high time she had a couple of
days off.'

'It seems a bit much, to disrupt the work at the bakery,
just to celebrate the arrival of a calf.'

'Maybe the calf's not the only reason.'

'Tell me another.'

Kay asked, but suddenly she did not want to hear his
answer.

'You'll find out at dinnertime, won't you?' York drawled,
and turning to Sam he invited, 'I'm going to feed the pony.
Are you coming?'

The abandoned icing had hardened in the nozzle, and the
irritation of unblocking it added to Kay's frustration. It was
just like York to enjoy keeping her in suspense. Well, for
once he should not have the satisfaction off getting his own
way, and enjoy watching the effect of his bombshell when
he condescended to drop it on her.

She would have a heart-to-heart talk with Helen as soon
as she arrived. Her sister had seemed oddly evasive
whenever they spoke on the telephone, concentrating on
talking about Sam and the business but, face to face, Kay
was confident she would learn the truth. Not that having

her fears confirmed would help any, but at least she would
not go in to dinner unprepared for York's announcement,
for surely that must be the other thing he had in mind to
celebrate.

To add to Kay's aggravation, Helen and Oliver did not
arrive until it was almost time to serve dinner.

The kitchen was a hive of activity, with waitresses
helping Kay to cut and plate, bustling in and out, and
turning her erstwhile sanctuary into much too public a
place to embark on any kind of personal discussion with her
sister.

Sam had had his meal earlier with Bess, and promptly
claimed the attention of his mother for his not-to-be-missed
bedtime story. Oliver went upstairs as well, and destroyed
Kay's last opportunity to corner Helen before the meal
began.

She dressed for dinner in a fever of anticipation and
dread, and scolded herself for both. This was not the first
time she had loved and lost, and she would survive it the
same as she had done before.

But this time it was different. Her love for York was of
the lasting kind. Experience showed her the difference, and
warned her of the bitter aftermath to follow.

Her hands shook uncontrollably as she zipped up her
dress, and added pearls at her neck and ears that were the
tears she refused to shed.

The watered silk of her gown was a rich green, a colour
appropriate to her feelings, she thought without humour, as
she made her way downstairs. As if in a dream—or a
nightmare—she took her now-accustomed place at the foot
of the table opposite to York, and felt like a usurper,
because this would be Helen's place from now on.

The guests were loud in their appreciation of her efforts.
Obliging York's wish for a celebratory meal, Kay had made
the table *en fête*, as well as the food. In a vain effort to stop
herself from thinking, she had spent any spare time not
taken up by actual cooking, in a whirl of activity round the
dinner table itself. Ruthlessly, she had unearthed all the
treasures Grand'mère used for her most sophisticated

entertaining. Tall, silver candelabra, that had taken the maids the best part of two hours to clean, glinted in the soft glow of the flames they held aloft. Water lilies, wrested from the lake in a raid that hurt Kay's conscience still, floated their alabaster beauty on low earthenware dishes, with here and there a bud vase holding aloft a few stems of freesias to give colour and height.

Kay thought she would hate the perfume of freesias for as long as she lived.

She had raided the cupboards for eggshell-fine china bowls of unearthly lustre, and goodness knew what antiquity, to serve as finger-bowls, and her heart wrenched as she remembered how she had destroyed a rose in order to float one of its petals on the water of each.

A red rose, for love. Her eyes closed in a brief shaft of agony.

She had pulled out all the stops to make the dinner perfect, and hoped hardily that she had made it memorable for York, as he had wanted it. Certainly, for a very different reason, it was a dinner she herself would never forget.

It dragged endlessly, and although Kay had prepared and cooked each dish herself, she was scarcely aware of what she ate. Course followed course in a seemingly interminable procession, while her seat at the other end of the long table from York—a position she had wished for so urgently at their first, intimately tabled meal—revealed its disadvantages more with every passing minute.

From it, she had only to lift her head to observe every slight movement York made. To see Helen sat beside him, his dark head bent towards her, and both of them smiling at something he said.

Oliver sat beside Kay, chatting about the swimmimng pool until she wished irritably that he would either be quiet or talk about something else. Then she felt instantly ashamed of herself, because of Sam.

The meal ended at last. Wine was replaced with the promised champagne, and an air of anticipation sharpened the attention of the guests. Amid much jocularity, York satisfied their curiosity.

'Sam's named the calf, so we can now drink to Prince.'
'Why Prince?'
'Because his mother's named Sheba, after the Queen, so Sam thought it would be a good name for him.'

Amid laughter and congratulations, they all drank to the new calf.

The talk and laughter died away, and York continued. 'There are two more reasons for us to celebrate tonight.'

Two? Kay's eyes flew up, startled, and locked with York's along the length of the table. The candle flames set devil lights dancing in their blackness, and her hand rose to clutch at the pearls about her throat. Why two more reasons? Was not one enough?

She felt grateful for the candles. Whatever they did to York's eyes, they threw long shadows too, sufficient, she hoped, to hide her cheeks, that by now rivalled the water lilies for pallor.

York's dark, hawklike face at the other end of the table mocked her bewilderment. He was cruel, playing with her as a cat plays with a mouse. Deliberately spinning out his announcement, in order to keep her in suspense. Kay's teeth gripped hard on her lower lip, and her tongue tasted the sharp saltiness of blood.

'Today, Oliver obtained planning permission for work to begin on the new swimming pool at the hospital. Digging will start on the foundations next Monday.'

So that was what Oliver had been talking about all through the meal? He must have wondered at her lack of interest, Kay realised numbly. He could not know that she had not registered a word he said.

'The third reason for a toast tonight . . .'

Kay went rigid. Her hands gripped the edges of the table, until it felt as if the impression of her white-knuckled fingers must be for ever indented on the ancient, iron-hard oak.

'The third reason is a cause for sadness, as well as for celebration.'

Kay willed herself to remain upright and unresponsive in her chair. Her spine felt stiff enough to crack but she dared not let go, or else it would become limp, like a rag doll, unable to support her.

How much more torture could she endure, before her nerves cracked, and she cried her agony out loud?

'You'll be glad to know that the gas leak has been mended at last. Which means our guests will be free to leave us tomorrow, and go back to the Melton to resume their interrupted holiday. So tonight's is a farewell dinner . . .'

Kay felt her head begin to swim. The faces circling the table receded, York's among them. The candle flames blurred, guttering into darkness, and a loud roaring sounded in Kay's ears.

Through it, she heard York say. 'So let's drink to our guests.'

Mechanically, her hand lifted her glass. The delicate crystal felt incredibly heavy, as if it was indeed made of lead, but somehow she managed to raise it to her lips.

The champagne stung the broken skin, and the small, sharp pain jolted Kay back again to her surroundings, the roar in her ears subsiding to a throbbing drum roll, that beat out the same message, again and again.

York had said nothing—not a word—about himself and Helen.

CHAPTER SEVEN

KAY was still no closer to discovering the reason for Helen's visit to Canon Court. Why had she come? And why for two nights? What was the *real* reason?

She heard Oliver say to the guests, 'Put your cases outside your room doors tomorrow morning. I'll have them picked up and put in the minibus, and you can re-occupy your rooms at the Melton as soon as we reach London.'

She would pre-empt the guests long before they had time to reach London, Kay planned silently. She would shake the dust of York's home from her feet, and re-occupy her room at the cottage. York and Helen could have Canon Court to themselves, and welcome!

No matter that Oliver's chef had the van. If she could not get a lift in the minibus, she would ring for a taxi. That would demonstrate clearly enough to York just how eager she was to remove herself from under his roof.

Beside her, Oliver was still talking.

'I thought it would be pleasant if we could all spend one last day together in London, and reverse our roles.' He smiled along the table at York. 'It would be a small thank you to York for his hospitality, and for so generously helping us all out of a difficulty.'

Generous . . . Kay's lips curled. York had exacted a price from Oliver that would almost pay for rebuilding the Melton, to say nothing of the price she herself had had to pay in lost peace of mind. There was no way she could itemise the cost of that, any more than she could write 'paid' on the final account, and forget about it when she left.

'The minibus will take your luggage to the Melton,' the hotelier went on, 'and I've hired a coach to carry us all off to London for the day tomorrow. We'll go part of the way by road, finish our journey on the river, and take in a theatre in the evening.'

His smile encompassed Helen.

'Helen will be coming with us. Her efforts have played no
small part in releasing Kay from their business, to help us
out here.'

So that was the excuse to bring Helen to Canon Court.
Oliver's proposed day out would certainly involve an early
start in the morning, and a late return after the theatre, and
it would have posed problems with baby-sitters; whereas
Bess would be more than willing to keep an eye on Sam
while Helen was out, leaving her free to enjoy the day with a
clear mind.

York had said it was time she had a day or two off-duty,
and this was his means of ensuring it. It was neatly
engineered, as were all of York's plans, Kay thought sourly.

An American voice boomed a toast. 'To Helen, and
Kay,' and she looked up, straight along the table to York.

His eyes said, 'Now you know!' And laughed at her as he
raised his glass in mocking salute.

Kay stared at him dazedly. Her mind felt as if it was
floating, but that might have been the champagne. Helen
looked happy and relaxed. There was a bloom about her
that Kay had not seen since the car crash, and she fixed a
smile on her own lips, and hoped desperately that her
misery did not show through.

Someone teased, 'Speech, Kay!' but dumbly Kay shook
her head. Her throat felt closed, and words would not come.

Oliver laughingly put his arm round her shoulders, and
said, 'Spare her. She's already said it all by giving us such a
marvellous meal. We'll show her how grateful we are
tomorrow.'

Unknowingly, he had blocked Kay's plan to quit Canon
Court for at least another day.

One more endless day before she could be free. Kay felt
despair settle on her, because no matter how soon, or how
far she travelled away from Canon Court, her heart would
remain behind her, for ever chained.

'What about Sam?' She made one last desperate bid to
extricate herself.

'Sam's already solved that one for himself.' York
overheard her, and finally snapped the trap shut. 'He's

spending the day with the stockman's son. I took him to see the calf on the way here this afternoon, and he can't wait to go back again.'

The rest of the evening passed in a whirl. Kay was given no oppportunity to speak to Helen on her own. The party stayed tightly bunched, as small parties tend to, and there was no chance of any private conversation as one or another of the guests remained stubbornly glued to Helen's side, with always Oliver or York there, too.

In the end, Kay gave up trying, and promised herself, 'Tomorrow, perhaps, when we're on the river.'

At the end of the evening Helen exclaimed. 'Isn't it warm? I must have a breath of fresh air before I go to bed.'

And before Kay could say, 'I'll come with you,' York cut in with, 'Come and do my nightly locking-up rounds with me.'

'I'd love that,' Helen said, and went out with him, and Kay retired, defeated. York's mention of locking-up rounds reminded her that she had left the kitchen window open to let out the steam, and she made her way to the now-deserted work room to close it in case it was one that York might miss.

Dusk had fallen, but there was still enough reflected glow from the sunset to enable Kay to see her way across the kitchen without recourse to artificial light, and she was reaching up a hand to pull the window shut when Helen and York strolled into view, going towards the stable block.

Helen's words came clearly to Kay's ears through the still-open window.

'No, York. Not yet. It's too soon after John. It's only just over twelve months since the accident.'

York stopped in an angle of the building, and Kay saw his hands reach out and draw Helen towards him.

'It's over eighteen months ago now, my dear,' he said, softly, but on the still night air the words carried to Kay's ears as clearly as if they had been shouted.

My dear ... She caught a quivering breath as York continued, 'Time, after all, is only relative. You've lived a lifetime of experience since your husband was killed. You've been through all the difficulties of starting up your own business, of coping with Sam's injuries, and teaching him to walk again. Don't throw away your own chance of happiness now.'

'It all seems to have happened so quickly.'

'But you're sure, in your own mind?'

'Oh, yes. I'm quite sure.'

The words were spoken low, but they were firm and very definite, and Kay's heart contracted.

'Then why wait, Helen?'

The pale cloud of Helen's dress blurred against the blackness of York's evening suit, and hurriedly Kay pulled the window shut on her sister's answer. She did not need to know any more. There would be no need for her now to seek a tête-à-tête with Helen on the morrow, and her heart felt like a stone inside her as she trudged upstairs to bed.

The next morning, York carried off an excited Sam in the pony and trap, reassuring the boy's mother, 'The groom will fetch him home to Bess in time for his tea.'

So Canon Court was 'home' to Sam already, Kay noticed bleakly, as she cooked breakfast.

Helen came in to help her, and promised gently, 'I'll do the breakfast tomorrow morning. You can have the day off.' As if she could not wait to take over.

It was Helen who sought her company for a chat now, and perversely Kay shrank from the confidences that she had been so eager to receive the day before. Later, when she felt strong enough to be able to control her own feelings, she would steel herself to listen, and make all the appropriate noises in reply.

But not now. Not yet. If she was to survive the day ahead, and come to the end of it with her secret still intact, she must have a little more grace in which to gather her resources.

She was aware of Helen's puzzled looks at her unusual lack of response, but she could not help it. Instead, she continued to find excuses to keep herself apart from her sister until the coach pulled up at the front door, and it was time for them to start off.

Kay took her seat without interest. They were to dine at the Melton, and a small case each for herself and Helen had gone on ahead with the guests' luggage, so that they could change for the theatre afterwards.

She hoped they would not have to share a room in which to change. If they did, she would not be able to avoid the confidences she sensed Helen was bursting to share, and she would be obliged to listen to her sister breaking what she would consider to be surprising news, and unknowingly twisting a knife in Kay's heart with every word she spoke.

She looked round nervously as York dropped on to the vacant seat beside her. She had assumed Oliver would come and take it.

'Oliver . . .?' she began.

'Oliver's coming, and so is Helen,' York answered casually, and sat tight. Kay shrank back against the window, and blessed the fact that the journey to where they were to pick up the river boat would be a comparatively short one.

Oliver followed with Helen, who smiled at York as she got on and took the window seat opposite, and the hotelier sat down beside her. Kay wished miserably she could change places with her sister, and it did not help to know that Helen must be wishing the same thing, just as fervently.

As the coach spun along the lanes, York began to point out various landmarks, but Kay felt too frozen to respond. After a while the message seemed to get through to him, and he turned and began to talk to Oliver on his other side instead, leaving Kay to her own dark thoughts.

York had said, 'Why wait?' So presumably that meant he and Helen planned to marry before very long. Perhaps they had even fixed the date while they were talking last night. It would explain Helen's eagerness to corner Kay this morning for a chat.

What would her own future hold afterwards? Kay wondered listlessly.

Helen would not want to continue working at the bakery after she was married, and between them they had succeeded in building up a business that was too much for one person to cope with alone for long.

After working so closely with Helen, the thought of

taking on a stranger as a partner was anathema to Kay. And, too, she would not want to remain at the cottage, so agonisingly accessible to Canon Court. However much she desired her sister to be happy, she could not bear to see Helen with York, to constantly be reminded . . . It would be better, for her own sake, if she made a clean break, and went right away.

But where to?

Oliver might offer a temporary lifebelt.

Kay's lips twisted wryly. She had left Oliver's employ because of one man, and she would go begging for him to allow her to return, because of another.

She would not be able to explain her reasons to Oliver this time, because she now knew he was a friend of York; and when she got together with the hotelier for their customary weekly business meetings, if he insisted upon swapping news of Helen and York, it would make any job with him untenable, too.

Their arrival at the river put a temporary end to Kay's heart-searching, and she left the coach with an overwhelming sense of relief. At least on the boat she would be free to move away from York.

It was conveniently moored at a landing-stage and, although it was a privately hired vessel and not a conventional river steamer, it was reassuringly large, with lots of open deck space.

Kay pretended not to notice the hand York held out to help her on board, and she gained the deck in an independent stride. Another few inches, and her short legs would not have been able to make it unaided, but by dint of pulling herself up by the rail she just managed it.

Lunch was laid out in buffet form, and she made straight for the table. She did not want the temptations on offer, but it gave her a convenient excuse to walk away from York, and she took her cup of tea and plate of food to balance on the boat rail, on the side of the deck furthest away from where he stood talking to Oliver.

Kay chose her meal carefully, with an eye to what the local waterfowl population would be most likely to dispose of, and under the pretence of eating, she crumbled the mixture into the water, and soon had a small flotilla of feathered diners swimming below.

The ducks liked the cream scones best, she noticed with a flash of amusement, A gooey mixture of cream and jam slid on her fingers, and caused a piece larger than the rest to slide into the water, and a noisy scuffle broke out as a brightly coloured drake grabbed it, and then had to fight off its companions as they tried to wrest the food from its beak.

To Kay's chagrin, the noise attracted York's attention.

'Feeding scones to the ducks is no way to treat Oliver's good lunch,' he chided, appearing beside her, and nearly causing Kay's cup and saucer to follow the cake into the water from her suddenly nerveless fingers.

With a convulsive grab she averted their fate, and said defensively, 'I'm only giving them a few crumbs.' And she ostentatiously licked her fingers clean of cream and jam to prove her point.

'From the smug look on the face of that little drake, I'd say he's had more of your lunch than you have.'

York's eyes were disconcertingly keen, and fixed unswervingly on her face, and Kay wished he would look back down at the ducks instead. His probing eyes X-rayed her mind, and she dared not allow him to read the thoughts that were flashing through it now because he was standing close beside her, his arm brushing against her own on the boat rail, paralysing it so that she could not move it away.

'I'll go and get you another scone to eat.'

'Don't bother, unless you want to feed it to the ducks yourself.'

'You didn't eat your lunch at the pub yesterday.'

'What I eat or don't eat has got nothing to do with you.' Kay's precarious hold on her nerves began to waver. 'If you must know, I had steak for my breakfast this morning, and I still feel full.'

His set face said he did not believe her, and Kay's mutinous scowl replied that she did not care.

His eyes glittered in the sunlight like black diamonds, and her heart began its all-too-familiar slow, painful thudding, that made her long to put up her hand to steady it; but if she did, York would see and guess the reason, so she kept her hand clenched at her side, that clenched tighter still when he growled, 'You're the most contrary female I've ever had to put up with.'

'It's a good job you won't have to put up with me much longer, then, isn't it?'

Oh, the agony of it, to throw such words at him like weapons, while her heart bled inside her because they were true. To staunch her own wound, she thrust again.

'If it wasn't for the risk of upsetting Oliver, I wouldn't be here now.'

'Where's so special, that you'd rather be there than here?'

'Back at the cottage, of course. Now the gas leak's mended, my obligation to Oliver is over.'

'Obligation? Is that how you looked at it? Has cooking a few meals at Canon Court been such a burden to you, in return for Oliver taking on the building of a whole new swimming-pool complex?'

'It's been a massive inconvenience. How would you feel if someone had blackmailed you into leaving your estate, and running another for an indefinite length of time?'

'If I'd known you felt like that about it . . .'

He did not know how she felt. He must not know. Kay's hand clenched itself round the shiny steel rail of the boat for support.

Would her mind for ever see comparisons like this, to remind her of York?

'If it wasn't for this trip, I'd be at the cottage now, getting things back to the way they were before.'

She nearly added, 'before you interfered in our lives,' but his look pierced her, and the words refused to come.

It was too late when he retorted, 'Things can never be the way they were before. They move on, and we've got to move with them, or else stagnate. People are like seeds. They either grow, or rot.'

He had said something similar to her once before, Kay thought vaguely, but she could not remember where, or when.

'Our business has been stagnating while I've been away. It was growing nicely before then.'

They glared at one another, their anger clashing in the

sunlight across the boat deck, and then Helen strolled
between them, and it was like the breaking of an electric
current as she leaned on the rail and said, 'Aren't the ducks
sweet? We'll all be able to feed them at close quarters soon.
Oliver says we can get off the boat when we come to the
lock gates, and walk along the towpath if we want to.'

'After the amount of food Kay's already given to them,'
York growled, 'if the ducks have any more, they'll sink.'
And snatching Kay's cup and saucer out of her limp grasp,
he strode back to replace them on the buffet table.

'Are you two still battling?' Helen gave Kay a searching
look, and made her feel instantly guilty, and then angry,
because Helen was blaming her, and not York. Anger was
her shield, which she could hide behind, and without it she
felt defenceless, unable to cope with something which was
rapidly growing beyond her meagre strength to control.

'Is anyone coming ashore?' Oliver called out, and Kay
looked round and saw that the boat was approaching the
dark cavern of a lock. It pulled in to the bank to allow them
to disembark, but this time there was no convenient
landing-stage to bridge the gap between the deck and the
shore, and Kay looked nervously at the long drop down to
the towpath.

Oliver helped Helen down, and they strolled on together,
and York reached up his hand to do the same for Kay.

'I'll manage.'

'It's too big a drop for you to make it on your own.'

'I'll jump.'

'If you do, you're more than likely to land in the water.'

With quick impatience York reached up and grabbed
Kay round her waist, and hoisted her bodily off the deck.

For a heart-stopping minute her feet hung suspended,
and she clutched wildly at his arms for support, and clung
on to them so tightly that when he deposited her beside him
on the turf, they refused to let go immediately. It was only
when he stood looking down quizzically at her, and asked,
'Was there something else?' that she remembered she still
had hold of him.

Her cheeks flushed a bright pink, and she released him
hurriedly, and gave him a flinty look when he commanded,

'Now for goodness' sake, call a truce for the rest of the day.'

'I don't know what you mean.'

'You know exactly what I mean. Put your cutlass back in its sheath, Katie, and stop fighting. Enjoy yourself. It's Oliver's treat today. Don't spoil it.'

He reached down, and before she could evade him he caught her hand in a firm grip. 'Come on. Oliver and Helen must be half-way to the next lock by now.'

And he must be longing to catch up with them. Electric impulses flowed up her arms from his fingers and goaded Kay into action. She forced her feet to twice their normal speed in the wake of the hotelier and her sister.

'What's your hurry?' To her surprise, York held her back. 'There's no need to rush. It'll take quite a time for the boat to get through the lock gates.'

'I thought you wanted to catch up with the others?'

'It's too hot to run. And besides, there isn't room on the towpath just here for four of us to walk abreast. We'll catch up with them soon enough where it widens out, further along.'

'There isn't room to walk in safety here.'

Kay was walking on the river side, where erosion had made deep bites into the soil of the bank, and nervously she edged further away from the water. The move brought her closer to York and he laughed, sliding his arm round her waist, and pulling her tightly in to his side.

'Don't worry. I won't let you drown.'

From the look on his face when he'd grabbed her from the deck of the boat, he had been tempted to do just that, but his expression now was relaxed, and he strolled beside Kay, matching his pace to her shorter stride so that she did not have to trot to keep up with him.

She could not decide whether it was paradise or purgatory, to feel the slow ripple of his muscles beneath the lightweight material of his summer clothes moving against her limbs in a sensuous massage that made her leg muscles feel weak, so that her steps became even more uncertain, and she stumbled over a tussock of grass.

Instantly York pulled her closer against him, preventing

her from falling. Kay caught her breath, and with the hand that was nearest to York, she gripped tightly on to the belt of her trouser-suit jacket, so strong was its urge to slide round his waist, and complete a dual link that would bind them tighter still.

She wondered briefly if Helen would mind seeing them together like this, if she happened to glance round. And knew she would not, any more than she had minded her late husband giving Kay a hug and a kiss in greeting when they met.

A stile confronted them, ending the towpath, which broadened out on the other side into a meandering footpath crossing a meadow gold with buttercups.

Mindful of their truce, Kay hesitated only briefly before allowing York to guide her over the shallow step, but she was unprepared for him tucking her under his arm again on the other side with a smiling, 'You're just a nice fit,' and strolling them along together at the same easy pace, still not attempting to catch up with the others, although there was more than enough room now for four to walk abreast.

Instead, York turned aside to where the gnarled branch of a willow tree hung low over the water, suggesting, 'Let's go and have a look. I promised Sam I'd let him know if there were any better minnows here than those in the river at home.'

'Sam would love it here.'

'We'll bring him one day,' York promised confidently. 'Now he's accepting rides in the pony and trap, it's only a matter of time before he'll accept riding in a car again. We'll use his fishing-net to entice him. Look, there are masses of minnows.'

By 'we' he meant himself and Helen. Kay tried without success not to let the difference hurt, for Sam's sake, and, pretending enthusiasm, she leaned with York over the hanging branch of the willow and gazed down into the water, meeting the sight of their own reflected faces, gazing back.

The sunlight struck glancing beams off the surface of the river, churned into tiny ripples as the shoal of minnows darted away from the ghostly apparitions so suddenly come to join them in the watery environment.

York laughed at their flight, and his teeth glinted white in the wavering reflection, his face turned towards Kay. She leaned over the willow branch, clutching tightly at the weather-scarred bark, and stared down at it, fascinated.

Was it only the ripples in the water that made the reflected face seem as if it was coming closer to her own? The ripples stilled, and it was not illusion, and she turned her head, startled, and her cheek brushed York's chin.

Swiftly, she ducked. She saw his hand come up as if to detain her, and with a frightened wriggle that copied the minnows for speed, she slid off the willow branch. It swayed alarmingly, and jettisoned her amid clumps of wild ladysmocks in the damp hollows underneath. Careless of the state of her shoes, she struggled back up the bank to the safety of the footpath.

In two strides, York joined her. 'What's the matter?'

'Nothing. I . . . looking down at the ripples makes me feel funny, that's all.'

What she felt was the opposite of funny, and she held herself stiffly apart from York as they resumed their stroll. She was aware of his glance probing her face, and to save herself from having to meet it, she stared down at her shoes, scuffing them in the buttercups until the toes were layered with pollen. The pure, bright gold of a wedding ring.

Kay's eyes blurred, and she bent hurriedly to trail a finger through the pollen dust, and said with unconscious wistfulness, 'Helen and I used to make a wish on the pollen, when we were little.'

'Try making one now,' York suggested and, stooping, he plucked a handful of the bright little cups and turned Kay to face him, holding them under her chin.

She jerked away from him nervously. 'Wishes don't work when you're grown-up.'

This one would not—could not—work, because she and Helen would both wish for the same thing; and while two women could love one man, it was not possible for both of them to win, and hold, that one man's love.

'Let's catch up with Helen and Oliver. I'll race you.' She spun away from York, ignoring his urgent, 'Wait, Kay!'

and drowning his call with her own cry of 'Cooee!' to make Helen turn, and stop.

She was breathless when she reached her goal, and she panted gaily, 'Beat you!' to York as he ran up behind her, as if it was a race for fun and not for flight.

Oliver smiled at her bright face, and asked, 'Are you enjoying your day, Kay?'

And Kay lied valiantly, 'Oh, yes. I'm loving every minute of it.'

York's eyes sought her sister. 'Are you enjoying it too, Helen?'

'I haven't enjoyed myself so much in ages,' Helen replied with a smile, and Kay watched their eyes meet significantly, and share their secret.

A secret which was no secret to Kay.

She had still not decided how to evade Helen's confidences by the time they reached the hotel, and her tension mounted as she walked into the familiar foyer.

'Hello, Kay!' the major-domo greeted her effusively. 'You're visiting your old stamping grounds, I see. Does this mean we can hope to have you with us again permanently?'

Sooner than you imagine, Kay thought darkly, but she merely smiled and made a non-committal answer, and the man continued, 'I'll let the staff know you're here. They'll be delighted to see you again.'

His welcome gave Kay just the escape route she was seeking.

The manageress of the hotel's hairdressing salon hurried to greet her as she mounted the stairs beside Helen to go to their room and change. As Kay feared, it was a shared room, and she urged the manageress impulsively, 'Come on in with us while we change, and bring me up to date with all the news since I left.'

Her ploy worked and, nothing loath, the older girl accompanied them, effectively preventing Helen from unburdening herself. As the three of them walked back downstairs again together, they were joined by Oliver and York at the foot, before the manageress could leave them on their own.

Kay could sense Helen's restless dissatisfaction that they

still had not managed any time alone together, and knew she would have to account for her avoidance later, when she finally ran out of excuses; but by then, she assured herself without much conviction, she would be strong enough to present a calm front when Helen divulged her news.

She was disconcerted to discover that the guests would not be dining with them as a party, but had dispersed to their own favourite tables in the restaurant, and she and Helen would be sharing a small table with York and Oliver, apart from the others, where they could converse in comfort.

It was the very opposite arrangement to what she herself would have chosen, and the burden of being obliged to carry her share of the conversation lay heavy on Kay.

No matter how hard she tried, her contribution at best was disjointed, her thoughts being constantly distracted by the smiles and soft glances Helen directed at York when she thought no one was looking, sending him messages which his own returning smile said he understood.

Oliver did not appear to notice, but to Kay's heightened sensitivity the exchanged glances were as obvious as if the two had hired the town crier to announce their love for one another.

'The cars are at the door, sir.'

The head waiter approached the table, and released her. To Kay's surprise, Oliver had elected to take them to the theatre in his own car, and a long, low limousine was pulled up behind it to convey the guests. Kay would have preferred the minibus, and the company of the whole party together.

Tensely she waited with Helen beside the Jaguar, and hoped Oliver would invite her to sit in the front with him, but, no doubt deferring to her sister's seniority, the hotelier opened the front passenger door and ushered Helen in beside him instead.

Woodenly Kay submitted to being helped into the back by York, who dropped in beside her and slammed the door shut.

The bright lights of Piccadilly mocked her, and she watched the streaming traffic with brooding eyes as Oliver took them to join it with a dextrous flip of the wheel.

York remarked, 'You're welcome to the wheel, among this lot.'

Oliver grimaced. 'I only brought the car tonight because we'll want it afterwards.'

Which meant they were going on somewhere else, after the theatre. Kay's heart sank. Would this day never come to an end?

Once, she herself had been part of the cosmopolitan stir and bustle of the capital, with people going places, herself among them. She had enjoyed every minute of it, then. Soon she would be returning to live that life again, and her whole being cried out in protest against the prospect.

All that she longed to do was to lean her throbbing head on her bedroom window-sill, and gaze out over fields that knew no other light than that of the sun and the moon, and listen for the call of the screech owl as it hunted for its supper.

She knew an overwhelming desire to lean her head on her arms and weep, right there in the car, because the bedroom window-sill of her thoughts was the one at Canon Court, and not the one at the cottage.

As they entered the theatre, and left their wraps at the desk, it crossed Kay's mind to wonder if Mervyn would be in the play being staged tonight. She knew a moment of misgiving as her eyes sought the placards on the walls of the foyer. Seeing Mervyn again would not upset her, but in her present mood, to be forced to endure a whole evening watching her ex-fiancé perform would add fuel to the growing sense of inadequacy that had dogged her all day.

Kay sighed. Would love ever work out for her? First Mervyn, and now York. Her searching eyes caught the relevant placard, announcing, 'Mexican Rhapsody, starring . . .'

She did not need to read any further. It was the current musical hit. A detached part of her mind told her that Oliver must have pulled strings, to be able to hire a box for them at such short notice, while the other relieved part

assured her, 'No Mervyn.' Whatever his personal opinion
of his own vocal prowess might be, nothing qualified the
actor to join the cast of this celebrated show!

The box was large and roomy, and accommodated the
whole party with ease, but it did nothing to help Kay's
situation, because when she sat down she found herself still
partnered by York. From her seat she had a perfect view of
the stage, but when the lights were lowered, she discovered
to her dismay that York's profile was still etched clearly
against the glow of the footlights.

Dancers came, banging tambourines and clicking casta-
nets, and diverted her attention for a brief, merciful
minute, but when the play got into its stride she discovered
to her dismay that the successful, up-to-the-minute musical
had as its theme the age-old dilemma of forbidden love.

With dismayed eyes, Kay watched the plot unfold.

She should not have come. Watching Mervyn would
have been better than this. Or even going to the
Hippodrome. This was too real. Too much. She gripped her
hands tightly in her lap, and felt the palms wet under her
fingers.

No matter that the baritone showed signs of rotundity,
and the soprano would never see her twenties again, their
voices were matured to their superb best, and with
superlative skill they drew their audience with them into
their own insoluble problem, singing out their longing with
a piercing beauty that sent arrows of fellow feeling shafting
through Kay's heart.

The singers agonised through song after song, the music
reached a climax of yearning and frustration, and Kay
ached with sympathy for their plight, which too clearly
mirrored her own.

Unbidden, the tears she was too proud to shed for herself
rose to her eyes for the two stage lovers, and she dabbed
cautiously with her handkerchief, terrified lest York should
notice, and scorning herself for her silliness, because the
story of the stage lovers would have a happy ending, which
was more than she could hope for her own.

'What's happened to the hard-boiled career girl I knew,
Katie?'

York *had* noticed. His voice was whispered laughter in her ear, mocking her furtive attempts to dry her eyes.

'Do you want to borrow my hanky?'

'*No!* Put it away,' she whispered desperately, as she saw his hand begin to reach towards his jacket pocket. If he humiliated her in front of the others, she would never forgive him.

'Never mind, Katie. It's only a play. It's just pretend.'

His hand was reality. It reached down in the darkness, and curled round her fingers, teasing out of their grasp the small, damp square of cambric, and substituting the warm comfort of his grip, that was no comfort at all to Kay.

She could feel his thumb slowly stroking up and down the fine purple veins on her wrist, and each slow stroke electrified her into a raw awareness of him, intensifying her perception of the singing that rose doubly heart-stirring to the ears, and threatened to turn the trickle of tears into an uncontrollable flood.

If they did, she would die of shame, and blame York for ever.

Frantically Kay tried to prise her hand free from his grasp, and he instantly tightened his grip. Gritting her teeth, she pulled. She dared not put too much pressure into the pull, for fear the others would notice, and York knew it and hung on.

'Loose me,' Kay hissed at him furiously.

'Did you say coffee, or tea?' York enquired urbanely. The curtain dropped for the interval, and the lights rose and brightened, and he loosed her hand and got to his feet, and goaded, 'Or do you need something stronger?'

Seething, she had no choice but to accept coffee and liqueurs, and the tiny, sweet biscuits that went with them, and felt furiously as if any one of them might choke her.

'There aren't any handy ducks here,' York remarked *sotto voce*, and Kay threw him a malevolent look, twisting down the unwanted food and drink past the blockage of anger that stopped her throat. She hated York for deliberately tormenting her. If he could taunt her like this now, what would he do if he suspected the secret of her love for him? Perhaps he did already suspect?

The thought nearly caused Kay to choke in real earnest, and she cringed into her chair as the lights dimmed once more, and the play resumed.

And York resumed his hold on her hand. He leaned over slightly towards her chair, so that she would not have to stretch out her arm to accommodate him, and the clean, astringent smell of his aftershave lotion caught on her breath as his face came unnervingly close to her own. His hand rested on her lap, and the weight of it felt as heavy as the weight of its owner's image on her heart.

The progress of the rest of the play escaped Kay. She was aware of the music, and the singing in the background, only as an accompaniment to the painful beating of her heart. Like the probe of a dentist's drill, that blots out all other sensation except the seat of the pain, she was aware only of the hard, determined clasp of York's hand round her own, and her surroundings were lost to her.

She was conscious of nothing and nobody but York, and was unprepared when he drew her to her feet, and joined with the cast and the audience in singing the National Anthem. As if in a daze she heard Oliver telling the guests that supper would be laid on at the Melton, awaiting their return.

He shook hands with the six, and to a chorus of goodbyes the limousine carried them away, and Oliver steered Helen towards the parked Jaguar.

'I thought they weren't flying home until Friday?' Kay said. 'Surely he'll see them again before they go?' It was only Tuesday now, and as Oliver lived in the penthouse flat above the Melton, he was bound to meet them as he went to and fro.

'Oliver's coming back to Canon Court with us,' York enlightened her.

'Wonders will never cease. To my knowledge, he hasn't had a day off since Tina died.'

'I told him it was high time he did.'

'And Oliver fell into line, and said yessir, just like that, I suppose? Do you manipulate everyone's lives regardless, as if you're some kind of despot?'

'Regardless of what?' York's eyes narrowed at Kay's sarcasm.

'Regardless of how they feel about it themselves. First, you prised me away from the bakery. Now, you're doing the same with Oliver.'

'Oliver's staff will keep his business running smoothly while he's away. And he doesn't look as if he's doing much objecting, does he?'

It was perfectly true. Oliver was laughing with Helen at something that obviously amused them both, and the hotelier's face was more carefree than Kay had seen it for a long time. York was quite right. Oliver had needed a break.

His very rightness served to fan the flame of Kay's annoyance even further. 'Do you always get your own way in everything, with everybody?'

'When my way happens to be the right one.'

'Your way isn't necessarily the right one for everybody.'

'In this case, it is.' York's voice hardened perceptibly. 'So don't try to interfere, Katie.'

'Interfere in what?' Kay snapped, and without waiting for him to answer, she hurried across to join Helen and Oliver by the car.

The hotelier asked considerately, 'Are either of you girls hungry?'

They both shook their heads. Helen looked too happy to be hungry, Kay thought dully. And she herself felt too miserable to want to eat.

'In that case, we might as well be going,' York suggested. 'Would you like me to drive back, Oliver?'

'A good idea.' The hotelier promptly relinquished his car keys into York's hand. 'You know the lanes better than I do, and you'll be able to take all the short cuts.'

Kay wished bleakly that she knew of a short cut out of her present situation. Oliver helped Helen into the back of the car, and joined her there. Which meant Kay was obliged to take the front passenger seat, where she had wanted to sit on the outward journey, and now felt she would do anything to relinquish, because it meant once more sitting beside York.

It was a silent journey back. Helen and Oliver seemed

content to remain without speaking in the back of the car, and although York made one or two desultory remarks, Kay pretended to be dozing beside him.

But although she shut her eyes, she was unable to shut away her thoughts, which continued to track round and round in her head in a hopeless circle that got no nearer to a solution the closer they got to Canon Court.

In vain, she assured herself, 'After tomorrow, it will all be over. I'll feel better about everything, after tomorrow, when I've left the Court and I don't have to see York every day.'

Yet she knew drearily that her spirit would never leave York's home, but would remain to haunt its ancient walls, like the pale ghost he had likened her to.

The car tyres crunched to a halt on gravel, and Kay opened her eyes and heard York say, 'Bess promised to leave us a snack in the kitchen. I wonder if she's remembered.'

'You can always resort to fish fingers. You've got plenty in the fridge,' Kay reminded him tartly, and pushed her way through the green baize door, hoping fervently that Bess had not forgotten. On top of the pain from a headache she had acquired, the smell of fish fingers being cooked would surely make her sick.

She switched on the light and saw silver covers lining the worktop, evidence that Bess had not forgotten. Helen said, 'I'll go upstairs and check on Sam before I eat,' and Oliver and York began to make instant coffee.

Their activities left Kay with nothing to do for the moment except to sink on to a stool, and wrestle with the poignant memories of that other late-night meal she shared with York, until wearily she wished she could despatch her memory, along with the fleeting hours that filled it, and be allowed to get on with the rest of her life with a mind swept clear of the past.

Helen came back with the report, 'He's sleeping like a lamb,' and Kay forced herself to her feet, and began to gather the dishes on to the table, investigating their contents incuriously.

The kettle whistled a warning, and Helen spooned coffee

granules into the mugs. Although it smelled good, Kay's nostrils rejected the aroma, and she wondered if it was because she and York had been alone in the kitchen before, that the perked coffee smelt so special to her.

She could feel his eyes on her as they sat down round the table, and defiantly she chose a couple of sandwiches she did not want, and managed to wash them down successfully with copious draughts of coffee.

The others seemed to be in no great haste to retire, and ate their supper in a leisurely manner while they discussed the merits of the play. Eventually Kay's silence registered with her companions. 'You look shattered, Kay,' Oliver said concernedly, noting the dark circles like bruises under her eyes.

'It's been a long day.'

It had been a lifetime long, and there were still the endless hours of the night to get through.

'We can all take it easy tomorrow,' York consoled, and Oliver rose to his feet and decided, 'I'll put the car away.'

'I'll call it a day, too.' Helen yawned and got up from her stool, and Kay's throat constricted. Helen would walk with her upstairs, and confide in her on the way, and she could not bear it tonight. Tomorrow, when she felt less tired, and her headache was gone. But not tonight.

Helen moved to join her, but York called out, 'Helen?' and her sister turned back. Kay hurried on alone along the corridor. After a while she heard the kitchen light click off and the door shut, and Helen and York walking behind her, but she did not wait, and they continued talking quietly together, making no effort to stop her from hurrying away.

Gripping the banisters with fingers that shook, Kay pulled her leaden feet step by step up the stairs, longing to run, but unable to summon up the energy to go any faster.

She felt desperately tired.

Her feet found the landing, and she stumbled along it towards her bedroom door. She tried to keep her eyes averted, but they seemed to possess a life of their own, and shafted downwards to where York and Helen stood at the bottom of the stairs.

Blindly, Kay reached for the knob of her bedroom door,

and thrust it open, but not before she heard York say, 'Have you come to a decision yet, Helen?'

And Helen answered, low-voiced, 'Yes, I've made my decision. I'll sleep on it, and let you know tomorrow. Goodnight, York.'

Standing on tiptoe, Helen reached up to kiss him.

Kay leaned back weakly against her bedroom door, trembling in every limb. She could hear Helen walking up the stairs. Her feet approached the door, and Kay drew in a difficult breath. In such a short space of time, she couldn't pretend to be asleep, if Helen knocked. But her sister's footsteps walked on, and a shudder of relief took Kay across the room to where she had longed to be all day.

The window was open to the warm night air, and she leaned her arms along the sill, and dropped her head down on to them, and let the tears flow.

But neither tears, nor the soft night breeze blowing from the darkened fields below, had the power to ease the anguish that racked her slender body with sobs.

Her head throbbed, and the delicate pulse in her temples beat with pitiless hammer blows, drumming one word over and over again through her cringing mind.

Tomorrow. Tomorrow.

CHAPTER EIGHT

HELEN's promise to cook breakfast gave Kay the perfect excuse to remain in her room until the gong sounded the next morning.

The summons quivered through her like an arrow, but she squared her shoulders and picked up her suitcase, which she had packed during the sleepless hours of the night. She gave a last, brief look round her bedroom, and her shoulders slumped as she closed the door behind her.

York was crossing the hall with Oliver when she walked downstairs, and Kay felt his hard glance latch on to her suitcase. With an effort she continued her descent as casually as her suddenly wobbly legs would allow her, deposited her case beside the front door, and replied to Oliver's cheerful, 'Good morning,' with, 'Can I beg a lift from you, to take me back to the cottage this morning?'

'Yes, of course.' The hotelier looked taken aback at her request. 'I didn't know you were going home today. I thought . . .'

Kay's brittle control wavered. 'I'm not a fixture at Canon Court.' She spoke more sharply than she intended, because she had nothing against Oliver.

'Is that Kay?' Helen's voice called out along the corridor. 'Come and help me to load the breakfasts on to the trolley.'

'This is it,' Kay told herself, and black despair closed over her.

She could not refuse to help Helen without causing comment. But if only her sisters tête-à-tête had come after breakfast, and not before, she could have escaped immediately afterwards, while now she would have to hear Helen out and still endure breakfast before she could get away.

With a thumping heart, she forced her dragging feet in the direction of the kitchen, while her nerves screamed out at them to run the other way.

'Wait for me, Aunty Kay! What's for breakfast? I'm starving.'

169

Kay could have wept with relief when Sam limped up behind her. Reaction made her lean down and give him a hug, which won her a puzzled look from the boy, while his mother sent her a rueful glance that said clearly, 'Foiled again!'

'We'll have to have a pow-wow later,' Helen said ruefully. 'It seems ages since we've been able to settle down to a good talk together.'

Kay nodded brightly and echoed, 'Later.' Grabbing the dishes, she bundled them on to the trolley and fairly ran it along the corridor towards the breakfast room before Sam could take it into his head to disappear again, and leave them on their own.

'What are we all doing today?' Helen enquired as she wielded the coffee pot.

'I'm going home,' Kay said, in a tight voice that defied anyone to contradict her.

She kept her eyes firmly lowered to her plate, and the silence in the room wrapped round her. Through it she could hear the loud ticking of the clock when for an endless minute no one spoke, until Sam piped up, 'I want to go and see the calf again. Can I, Uncle York?'

Kay raised her eyes then, and saw York nod his assent to the child, but his eyes were fixed on herself, and she steeled herself to meet his look with a calm indifference that was belied by the suffocating beat of her heart.

Oliver said, 'I've got to go and see an architect this morning,' and mercifully distracted York's attention, and Kay felt weak when his eyes exchanged her face for that of the hotelier as Oliver added, 'I'm expecting a phone call, to tell me the time of the appointment. Shall I answer it when it rings, York?'

Oliver's appointment with the architect would be about the swimming pool. Work was to start on it next week, Kay remembered.

Which left Helen and York on their own.

It was all falling into place like a jigsaw puzzle, Kay thought, and felt her nerves vibrate as the telephone shrilled its clarion warning from the hall.

'That'll be the man now, I expect,' Oliver said, and

disappeared to answer it. He left the door open behind him, and his voice floated back to the breakfast room.

'In about half an hour? No, it's not too soon for me. I'll meet you there.'

'I'll go with him,' Kay promised herself silently. Oliver could drop her off at the cottage, and an hour or two there on her own would give her time to regain her poise before Helen caught up with her.

Oliver swung back into the room and said to Helen, 'You'll have to come in the car with me. There won't be time for you to go in the pony and trap.'

His step was jaunty, and Kay thought, 'What a difference the interest of the swimming pool has made to him.'

'Do I have to go as well?' Helen asked.

'He'll expect us both. You were in on the initial talks about the pool.'

'I'll go and get my coat.'

Kay rose too. 'It looks as if you're going to be on your own,' she said sweetly to York as she passed him, and mocked the American's invariable farewell, 'Have a nice day.'

'I intend to,' York retorted, and called after Oliver, 'You take the suitcase in the boot of your car, Oliver. Kay's coming in the trap with me.'

'I'm doing nothing of the sort!' Kay snapped. She rounded on him, her eyes flashing. He was doing it again. Dictating what she should or should not do. Sublimely confident that she would fall in with his wishes, regardless of what her own might be. 'I'm going with Oliver.'

'*Helen's* going with Oliver.' York's eyes were hard on her face, and Kay was reminded uncomfortably of his odd command in the car park last night. 'Don't interfere.'

What did he mean, with his imperious orders? she wondered sarcastically. It could not be with the swimming pool discussions. They were as much her concern as anyone's.

'Sam can't travel in the car, so he'll need you along with him in the trap.'

Sam reinforced this argument by slipping his small paw through Kay's hand, and begging her anxiously, 'You'll come and see the calf with me, won't you, Aunty Kay?' and she felt her resolve begin to weaken. '*Please*, Aunty Kay?'

Kay let out her breath in an exasperated rush. 'Oh, all right. The farm's on the way home, anyway.' And hated the undisguised triumph in York's expression as he turned aside and said to Oliver, 'We'll see you at the cottage later.'

He seemed to be in no great hurry to learn what it was Helen had to tell him today, Kay brooded. Had her sister already told him of her decision? But if so, why did they not announce their engagement?

Perhaps Helen preferred to wait until she had told Kay first, privately. The glow on her sister's face said that Helen could not have changed her mind.

Kay watched the Jaguar disappear along the park drive, and walked reluctantly with Sam to the trap. To balance the vehicle, with only two adults aboard instead of three, York got in and sat sideways in the front, facing Kay, and she shifted uncomfortably in her seat, not knowing where to look.

Always before he had sat centrally in front with his back conveniently turned towards herself and Helen, and he grinned at her open astonishment when Sam took up the reins and with a practised click of his tongue, set the pony in motion.

'Sam, ought you to . . .?' Kay began nervously.

'Don't fuss. He enjoys driving. He'll make a good carriage driver when he grows up. He's got perfect hands.'

'He's not grown-up yet. He's only six, and he's too little.'

'He's seven next month, and too old for apron strings.'

Kay flushed a dull red, but before she could let fly the angry rejoinder that sprang to her lips, Sam threw carelessly over his shoulder, in a grown-up sounding voice that under any other circumstances would have made her smile, 'Don't be afraid, Aunty Kay. I only drive in the park. Uncle York says I've got to grow to over five feet tall before I can take the trap on the road by myself.'

York had got an answer to everything.

Kay relapsed into simmering silence. If Sam was willing to accept his continuing dictates, he would discover that she was not. With compressed lips she fixed her eyes on the briskly trotting pony, and tried to suppress an uprush of pride in Sam's unexpected achievement.

He was a different child from the nervous little creature of a few short weeks ago, and although he still limped as badly as ever, Oliver expected the swimming pool to be opened before the end of the summer, so there was hope in that direction, too. The future—for Sam—looked bright.

But there was such a thing as pushing the boy too far, too fast, Kay decided angrily, and the moment Sam was out of earshot, she would let York know how she felt about his pushing, in no uncertain terms.

The lark sang overhead again, but Eden seemed further away from Kay than ever, and even the calf, when they reached the farm, had lost its first dewy innocence that had so endeared it to Kay, and refused to come to suck her fingers, as it had done before.

Instead, when she put her hands through the rails, it bounced away out of reach, and frisked round the enclosure on legs already grown sturdy, and kept a wary eye on its human admirers as it nuzzled its mother for milk.

Things can never be the way they were before . . .

It was almost as if York had repeated his words out loud. They were so clear in her head that Kay turned instinctively to glance up into his face, and met his enigmatic look that said the words all over again, taunting her inability to make time stand still.

'The calf won't play.' Sam echoed her own disappointment, but York was swift to console him. He was invariably kind to the child, she thought, with a sudden stab of envy.

'Calves grow up quicker than children. He'll go out in the field tomorrow with the rest of the herd, and play with the other calves there. You'll be able to watch them, but they'll be too rough for you to join in.'

'Now who's holding apron strings?' Kay murmured maliciously.

York shot her a steely look, but instead of replying, he turned again to the child and said, 'Let's go on to the the next farm. I've got something there to show you that's more interesting than a calf.'

The puppy.

Kay drew in a hissing breath. She did not need York to tell

her out loud what it was, and he would not just be showing it
to Sam, she guessed. He intended to give it to the boy now, in
her presence, no matter what she had said about him not
being able to have a puppy at the bakery.

Was this why York had insisted upon her coming with
them, in the pony and trap, in order to demonstrate his
power to thwart her in everything she said and did? To
demonstrate that he would not allow her to interfere?

'Uncle York! Help!'

Sam's urgent shout, and the sudden, uneven clatter of the
pony's hooves jerked Kay back to consciousness of her
surroundings. She looked round her, startled.

'What's the matter? What . . .?'

York's calm voice cut across her rising cry. 'There's no
need to panic. The pony's cast a shoe, that's all. I'll take the
reins now, Sam, and walk him to the barn. We'll have to get
the farrier to fix him up with another.'

The barn. Kay had not realised they were so close to the
second farm. She stared at the building with apprehensive
eyes as York drew the pony to a halt beside it. How many
turkeys, if any, were still left inside?

She averted her eyes, and forced her feet to follow York
towards the house. The farm manager met them on the
doorstep, and when York explained what had happened the
man offered amiably, 'I'll go and unhitch the trap for you,
and turn the pony loose. Then I'll ring the farrier.'

'Come in and have a snack while you're waiting, Mr
York,' the manager's wife invited from inside the house, and
for the second time Kay was confronted by the sight of a
massive bake-up in progress on the white, scrubbed table.

The woman's greeting to Kay was friendly, if not effusive,
and she thought wonderingly, 'These people grow on you.'

Sam had no doubts about his welcome. He squatted
happily on the hearthrug, and accepted a jam tart and a glass
of milk with a grin of thanks that brought an answering
smile to warm the woman's face.

'The dogs will be in soon,' she told him, and Kay thought,
she knew we were coming, and why. York had it already
planned.

Her ire rose at this further evidence of his cunning

manipulation of circumstances and people, in order to drive them like sheep in the way he wanted them to go. If they did not fit in with his plans, he simply cut them to size until they did, and the sharpness of his shaping smarted as Kay sipped her cup of tea, and waited fatalistically for the dogs to put in an appearance.

The adult Jack Russell came and took its accustomed place near the table in the hope of falling titbits, but when the pup followed, it hurtled its small body straight at the child, as if it, too, knew exactly why he had come.

It wriggled and licked and bounced with seemingly inexhaustible energy, and Sam was clearly enchanted. He burst into helpless giggles at the pup's baby efforts to produce a bark, and the two rolled together on the rug in an inextricable tangle of fun as if they had been waiting for one another all their lives.

'Can I come and play with him again?' Sam begged, with his arms full of puppy.

'You can take him home with you, if you want him. I'll be right glad to get him out from under my feet.' The smile on the woman's face belied the severity of her words, and Sam's eyes grew round.

'Can I really? *Can I*, Aunty Kay?'

His small face shone, and Kay felt a lump rise in her throat as she watched him. The puppy was Sam's Eden. And York had deliberately engineered it so that it was she who had to open the door and let him in, or slam it shut in his face.

He was cruel. *Cruel!* Her tormented eyes flung the accusation at him with bitter condemnation. And then she looked back at Sam, and knew she could not be the one to deny him the puppy.

Soon, Helen would be married to York, and she and Sam would leave the bakery. And until then, they would manage somehow to keep the puppy and the bakery separate. How, she had no idea, but it would not be for very long.

That being so, why could York not have waited for another week or two, until they were all living together at Canon Court, and the animal would have caused no problems? But no, that was not York's way. He had to do it

now, and show his authority over her. Kay's face was tight as
she looked at him.

'Aunty Kay?' Sam's voice was an anguished plea from the
rug.

Kay drew in a deep breath. 'Yes, if your mother agrees,'
she prevaricated.

She refused to capitulate completely, and give York the
satisfaction he was looking for, but to Sam her guarded
permission was enough. He jumped to his feet and made
what haste his crippled leg allowed him to the door, and the
puppy blundered after him, following its future.

Would that her own might be so clear cut, Kay thought
bleakly.

His goal achieved, York rose, too. 'I'll go and find Jim,
and see if he's had any luck with the farrier. Coming, Kay?'

'Just try to stop me,' she muttered.

Wherever Sam was, there she intended to remain herself
until she handed the boy over to Helen. She did not trust
York. Without her presence, she could not tell what he might
push Sam into doing next.

He outstrode her into the farmyard, and when she caught
up with him he was speaking to the farm manager. York
turned as Kay came up to him.

'The farrier can't come until tomorrow.'

It took several seconds for the implications of what he said
to register in Kay's mind.

'That means we can't use the pony?'

'Not with one of its shoes missing.'

Kay gave a convulsive swallow. What she had dreaded,
ever since York began to take them out in the pony and trap,
had happened. Without the accustomed transport, how were
they to get Sam home? It was impossible for the boy to walk.

This was all York's doing, and Kay rounded on him.

'You're making it up. You're just saying this to . . .'

'It's true, miss,' the farm manager intervened. 'The
farrier . . .'

'The farrier must have *some* time to spare before the end of
the day. He can't possibly be busy every single minute.'

'It'll be gone midnight before he gets back, I expect, miss.
He's on duty all day at the race course, and it's a long drive

home after the racing's finished, and that won't be until late afternoon.'

It was true. The nightmare was actually happening. She turned on York furiously.

'Now see what *your* interference has done,' she blazed. 'Are you satisfied, now you've . . .?'

'Don't get so upset, Katie.' York's hand reached out and took her arm.

'Don't get upset?' She wrenched her arm free. 'How are we to get him home?'

'We'll try him in the Land Rover.'

'You must be joking.' Kay stared at him as if he was talking in a foreign language. 'It's Sam who'll be upset, if you try to make him ride in a vehicle. I won't *let* you make him,' she declared vehemently. 'You haven't seen him panic like I have. And I've had to help cope with what comes afterwards. The nights of screaming and crying with nightmares, and tummy upsets that have brought his weight down to half of what it ought to be. And *you* tell *me* not to get upset?'

She was perilously close to tears. Somehow, she had to get through to York, to prevent all the dreadful traumas of the months after the car crash from starting up all over again. For Sam's sake, she was even prepared to lower her flag and beg.

'York, please listen.'

She might as well try to talk to a brick wall, she thought despairingly. The farm manager drove the Land Rover out of the barn, and braked it to a halt close to where they stood. It looked different, and Kay saw that the top had been stripped off until it was little more than an open shell of a vehicle. A mechanised replica, in fact, of the trap.

'York, please listen,' she pleaded.

But York was turning away, and hunkering down beside Sam, who trotted up with the puppy cradled in his arms. For the moment the little animal had had enough of play, and was curled up drowsily, half asleep, chewing the end of Sam's jersey sleeve.

'We can't use the pony until tomorrow, Sam.' York had no inhibitions about loading the problem on to six-year-old shoulders, Kay thought contemptuously, and tensed as Sam considered the situation gravely for a minute or two, then presented it from his point of view.

'My puppy can't walk home. His legs aren't long enough.'

'You could leave him here at the farm for another day or two.'

'No! I want to take him with me.'

Small arms clutched more tightly round the newly acquired treasure, and Sam's freckled face became mutinous. Kay's heart sank. The little lad could be as stubborn as a mule when he set his mind to it. Without much hope, she tried to reason with him.

'But Sam, darling . . .'

'I want to take him with me.'

'We could take him in the Land Rover.' York nodded casually to the stripped-down vehicle, and Kay drew in a hard breath.

How could he? How *dared* he?

'You'll have to cuddle him all the way if we do, because he's never had a ride in a Land Rover before. But if you hold on to him, and Glen sits in front of you, like he always does, you should be able to get him home all right.'

He dangled his carrot in front of the boy, and left him to decide whether or not to take it. The child looked from the puppy to York, and from York to the Land Rover—a long, serious look that seemed to go on for ever, and Kay felt her stomach tighten into a hard knot inside her.

There was an endless pause. York waited for Sam to make up his mind, as if there was all the time in the world.

At last Sam looked up, and Kay wanted to shut her ears against what must come next.

'You'll have to lift me into the Land Rover, Uncle York. The step's too high, and I can't loose the puppy.'

The world began to waver in front of Kay's eyes. The face of the farm manager, the two faces so close together beside her. Kay blinked hard, and brought the world back into focus again, and heard York say, 'Tell Glen to jump up first, the same as you always do.'

The same as he always did. He was likening the Land Rover to the trap, as if there was no difference, and Sam was falling for his ploy. But when the engine started up, the child would feel the difference, and then . . .

'Get up, Glen.'

Obedient to Sam's command, the Rottweiler scrambled up into the high vehicle, and York bent and scooped boy and puppy into his arms.

Over the child's head, his eyes met Kay's, but instead of the triumph she expected to see in them, an odd expression fired the black orbs. It seemed to reach out to her. Commanding her.

Kay blinked, and looked more closely, but the expression was still there. Demanding something of her. But what?

A trembling started in the base of her throat. She tried to speak, to ask what it was York wanted of her. But no words came, and York turned and lifted the boy gently on to the seat, and told him, 'Wriggle along, and leave room for your Aunty Kay.'

He handed Kay up beside Sam, and keyed the engine into life, and said matter-of-factly to Sam, 'Have you got hold of Glen's collar? Don't make him feel jealous of the puppy.' And very slowly, he set the vehicle in motion, and crawled it out of the farmyard.

Kay dared not look at Sam. She hardly dared to breath. A tight band seemed to constrict her chest, suffocating her, and the trembling spread through her limbs, making her feel weak all over.

This was not happening, Kay thought. She was dreaming, and any minute now she was going to wake up, and find it was not true. And it had to be true. It had to be, for Sam's sake.

The tyres met the smooth tarmac of the park road, but still York kept the speed of the vehicle down, and still Sam remained engrossed with the puppy. By now its teeth had turned the cuff of the boy's jersey into soggy ribbons, but Kay dared not remove it out of reach for fear of distracting Sam into a realisation of what was happening to him.

The vehicle rolled on its way, and York said easily, 'What are you going to call the pup, Sam? You'll have to give him a name.'

'I haven't thought.'

'Think of one now, before you get home, and then you'll

have it ready to tell your mother and Uncle Oliver. What do you think would be a good name for the puppy, Katie?'

York pulled her into the conversation willy-nilly, demanding that she behave as if nothing unusual was happening, and the challenge in his look rallied Kay's scattered wits, and she said the first name that entered her head.

'Sally?' The catch in her voice was suspiciously like a sob.

Sam giggled, and the merry peal was like music in Kay's ears. 'Sally's a girl's name. My puppy's a boy. Uncle York said so.'

And of course, whatever York said was gospel.

'Try another,' he suggested, and Kay flashed back, 'You try. It's your turn now.'

'Horatio? How will that do, Sam?'

They played the name game all the way back to the cottage, distracting Sam's attention away from the fact that he was riding in a vehicle. Innocent of their ulterior motive, the boy joined in, and they bounced names about like ping-pong balls, vying with each other to find the most outrageous one.

Kay laughed and guessed names as brightly as the others, but hers was a brittle gaiety that felt as if it must snap if the journey continued for much longer, and the brightness in her died like a blown-out candle flame as Sam announced, 'I think I'll call him Gyp. I like that one best,' and York drew the vehicle to a halt at the cottage gate.

Helen and Oliver were sitting on the lawn, and at the sight of the Land Rover Helen hurried over to the gate, her face anxious. It was a study in conflicting emotions when York turned and lifted the boy down to join her.

He put a swift, warning finger to his lips as Helen started to speak, and cut across her words with, 'The pony cast a shoe.' Casually, as if it was the most natural thing in the world to use the Land Rover instead.

Helen's eyes were swimming as she stared from York to the child, and Kay doubted if she could see whether the puppy was a Jack Russell or a Labrador, as Sam held it up for her inspection.

'I've called him Gyp. Aunty Kay says I can keep him.'

York laughed, easing the tension. 'That boy will be a

diplomat when he grows up. He's already learned how to twist you two round his little finger, to get his own way.'

'He's had expert tuition just lately,' Kay bit out, and the tension was back again, but Helen was too starry-eyed to notice. She watched her son limp into the cottage to find a box for his pet's bed, and then she looked back at York, and breathed, 'I don't know how to thank you, for what you've done for Sam.'

York would shortly get his reward, Kay thought sourly, and maintained a stony silence as Helen went on, 'First you, and now Oliver with the swimming pool. Between you, all the past dreadful months will soon be nothing but a bad memory for Sam.'

Kay had been their mainstay through those dreadful months. Had Helen forgotten? Or was her sister ready to relegate her among the bad memories, in the face of their new and brighter future? In spite of herself, Kay's lips trembled.

She felt York's eyes fix themselves on her face, and hurriedly she turned her head aside.

'Kay had a hand in it, too,' York said perceptively, and Helen reached out an arm and put it across her sister's shoulders.

'Neither Sam nor I could have survived without Kay. But I don't have to tell her that. She already knows,' she said, and her arm tightened in a hug that was almost Kay's undoing.

'I'll go and unpack my suitcase,' she said hurriedly.

'Oh, my goodness.' Oliver looked conscience-stricken. 'Kay, I'm sorry. I left your case at Canon Court. I'd got such a lot on my mind when Helen and I left, I clean forgot about it.'

'I'll take Kay back to the Court to fetch her case,' York offered.

'You can bring it some other time. Send it by the groom,' Kay declined hastily, but York was already steering her back into the Land Rover.

Helen said, 'By the time you get back I'll have lunch ready. We can talk then.' And she disappeared, with Oliver in tow.

Kay grumbled as she resumed her seat in the Land Rover. 'By the time I've finished going backwards and forwards to

Canon Court, I'll feel like a yo-yo.'

But York disregarded her complaint, and sped the vehicle away from the cottage at three times the speed he had driven before.

'Is it too breezy for you?' he asked, as Kay put up a hand to her wind-tossed hair. 'I can put the hood up now, if you'd prefer it?'

'No. I like it better open.'

'While the weather stays hot, I'll use it as often as possible to take Sam around in.'

Kay sent him a guarded look. 'I suppose I ought to thank you for that,' she admitted grudgingly. 'You were right. About getting him to ride in the Land Rover, I mean. I suppose Helen and I have been a bit over-protective.'

'It was natural under the circumstances. You've all been through a very bad time, and now things are beginning to improve, you want them to stay that way. Anybody would do the same, in your shoes.'

'It was a good idea, stripping away the hood and the side-screens.'

It had been a brilliant idea, but she had no intention of overdoing the kudos. She had acknowledged her gratitude, and that was enough.

'Helen told me Sam had to be cut out of the wreckage of his father's car. Apparently the roof folded in on top of them.'

Kay gave a silent nod, and York's face held quick compassion, but he went on matter-of-factly, 'An open-topped vehicle won't hold the same feeling of claustrophobia for him, and by the time winter comes, and we have to use the hood again, hopefully he'll be so used to the Land Rover that he won't take any notice.'

'You've got an answer for everything.'

Except the one her heart longed to hear. The last chapter of the book was beginning to unfold, and Kay felt like a puppet, moving woodenly through the pages, dancing to the pull of other people's strings.

The Land Rover slowed, and York swung it off the road into a field gateway under some trees, and Kay said with forced brightness, 'Don't say this thing's thrown a shoe, as well?'

She felt proud of her attempt at humour. While she could pretend to laugh at the world, no one need ever suspect what lay beneath her smile.

'There's nothing wrong with the Land Rover. I want to talk with you.'

A quiver passed through Kay, and her hands gripped tightly together on her lap. Was York going to tell her himself, because Helen was constantly being interrupted, and he had got tired of the delay in announcing their plans, and determined to take matters into his own hands?

She gripped her fingers together until the knuckles showed white, but she forced her lips into a smile, and her voice to say lightly, 'Everyone seems to want to talk to me. First Helen, and now you. It'll be Oliver next. He must have something weighing pretty heavily on his mind. I've never known him to forget anything before. The swimming pool shouldn't worry him that much. He handles bigger problems every day of his life. If he finds it too time-consuming, why doesn't he leave it to the architect to deal with?'

Nerves made Kay chatter, even at the eleventh hour trying to delay what she knew to be inevitable, but York remained silent, and her voice faltered to a stop.

'The architect didn't want to see Oliver about the swimming pool.'

'But I thought . . .?'

'So did Helen.' York's lips lifted. 'The architect wanted to meet Oliver to give him the results of a survey on a house he's interested in, near here.'

'A house? What does Oliver want with a house? He's got the penthouse flat over the Melton.'

'That was fine while he was alone. But it's no place for a wife and child. He's going to turn it into an office.'

'Oliver? A wife and child?' Kay stared at York, stunned. 'Who . . .?'

'You must have noticed what's been going on between Helen and Oliver, ever since the day of the wedding?'

'Helen . . . and *Oliver*?'

Kay repeated the words stupidly, as if saying them out

loud might make them make sense.

'Of course. Why else do you imagine I spent so much time taking Sam out fishing recently? We've practically emptied the river of minnows. But it was the only way to give Helen and Oliver some time on their own. When Helen walked into the house on the morning of Louise's wedding, Oliver fell head over heels in love with her, and he'll never recover. When Helen told me she felt the same, I had to do my bit in giving their romance a chance to blossom.'

'Helen told you? She didn't say anything to me.'

'You didn't give her a chance. You've been as elusive as a will o' the wisp. Which was why she was forced to turn to me to confide in.'

'I'm sure you gave her good advice.' Kay's sarcasm lacked its usual edge.

'I simply asked her if she was sure of her own feelings, and when she said she was, I suggested there was no point in her waiting.'

Kay had heard him tell her, but that was a secret that must for ever remain buried, with all the heartbreak that went with it.

'Did you really have no idea what was going on? Couldn't you see the difference in your own sister?'

'Of course I could.' Kay came to life, stung that York should think her so insensitive. 'But I thought . . . I thought . . .' She ground to a halt. She could not tell York, of all people what it was she thought.

'What did you think, Katie?'

York's hands reached out and cupped Kay's face, turning it towards him so that she could not look away. Her colour ebbed and flowed under his touch, and she felt her mind go numb, incapable of rational thought while his fingers signalled messages to her heart that made it thump until it brought a lump to her throat.

She longed to turn her head and press her lips to his fingers, that stroked lines of fire across her forehead as he reached up and gently pushed aside wind-blown tendrils of hair from her face.

'Tell me, Katie,' he insisted.

'It doesn't matter,' she mumbled.

'It matters a lot, to me.'

The antics of her heart were making her dizzy. It reacted like a barometer before her mind had time to grasp the meaning behind his words. The pulse at her temples took up the beat, the delicate blue veins talking to the slim, tanned fingers that covered them, and Kay felt them go tense as they listened to the message. She caught her breath. Had they understood?

'Tell me, Katie.'

He tipped up her face still further, forcing her to meet his eyes, and the look of determination in them told her he would not let her go until she gave him an answer.

'I thought . . . Helen and you . . .' She could not go any further.

'Helen and me?'

Conflicting emotions chased one another across York's face. Astonishment, and growing understanding, and a faint, dawning hope that lit his eyes with twin flames. They wavered and struggled, and then burst into bright, glowing life.

'Katie, Katie,' he groaned. 'What shall I do with you?'

His hands left her face, but it stayed upturned to his as if fixed, while his arms went round her, and drew her close against him.

'What shall I do with you?'

'Marry me,' her heart cried, but her mouth could not form the words, because York's lips were claiming it for their own, and for a timeless moment she was locked in his fierce embrace.

'Helen's in love with Oliver, not me,' he murmured in her ear, 'although,' a laugh threaded through his voice, 'although she did mention that she wouldn't mind having me for a brother-in-law.' York's arms tightened, and his voice became hoarse.

'It's you I love, not Helen. That's why I kept coming back to the cottage week after week. I was the moth, and you were the flame that drew me. And when I had to keep going after the wedding was over, and leave you behind to cook dinner for the guests, I hated them for being at the Court. I felt as if I was being torn in two, having to leave you.'

His voice tightened as if under an unbearable strain. 'I love you, Katie. I want you. I need you. Will you marry me? I've tried so hard to hold back, not to rush you. But I must know. I can't wait any longer.'

His words were broken and disjointed, but they reached Kay's disbelieving ears like music, and she felt the ice inside her melt.

From somewhere high above them a lark began to carol. Another joined in, and then another, until the whole sky seemed to be full of their singing, the music throbbing from tiny throats like a fanfare, beckoning Kay into her Eden.

'Give me some hope, Katie?'

York mistook her silence, and his voice pleaded. His face had taken on a curiously grey tinge under its healthy tan.

'Don't leave me in suspense,' he begged hoarsely. 'At least tell me if I have a chance with you? If you hate the thought of having stock on the farms so much, I'll get rid of it all, and grow crops and flowers instead. You were so upset about the turkeys. That's why I took them to Helen instead. But I'll get rid of the flock, and the cattle . . .'

'No, York. No.'

He drew back, and his eyes held an anguish that would live with Kay for ever.

'Is that your last word, Katie? Is there no chance that you'll ever change your mind, and learn to love me?'

His lips had turned as grey as his face, and Kay reached up swiftly with her own to bring back the bright, healthy colour flowing into them again.

'I love you now. I'll always love you,' she whispered. 'I meant no, don't get rid of the herd. Not no, I won't marry you.'

Her words tumbled over one another, incoherent and confused, but the glow that lit York's eyes said he understood, and her voice faded into silence under the eager, demanding ecstasy of his kiss, that sealed their love for a lifetime and beyond, while the larks carolled on, and time stood still.

Endless weeks of passion he could no longer suppress spent themselves in York's kisses, and at last, her face flushed and her eyes sparkling, Kay lay back in his arms.

'Promise me you won't get rid of the herd? They're the realisation of your dream.'

'*You're* the realisation of my dream. I've dreamed of nothing else, ever since you stepped out of Louise's car that Sunday afternoon, when you first came to Canon Court. Your eyes were like pansies. I wanted them to grow in my garden, for me and no one else.'

'You tried your best to get rid of me.'

'I didn't want you to work for me, even as a caterer. I wanted you for my wife. Then I realised if I could blackmail you into working at the Court, I could see you every day. I couldn't resist the temptation. Forgive me?'

Kay forgave him in the most convincing way she knew.

'Helen and I won't be catering for much longer,' she realised without regret. 'We'll have to sell the bakery.'

'Oliver's got a prospective buyer.'

'Already? He hasn't lost much time.'

'He didn't need to advertise. The chef who's been helping Helen while you've been at the Court wants it for himself and his son, who's a chef as well. They're both keen on having a small business which they can run together.'

'You've got an answer for everything,' Kay teased.

'You've just given me the only answer I want,' York said, and drew her hungrily back into his arms.

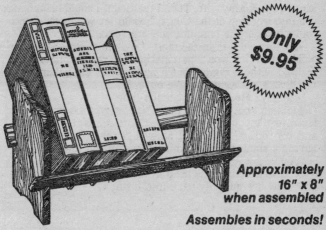

Can you keep a secret?

You can keep this one plus 4 free novels

MAIL-IN-OFFER
OFFER CERTIFICATE ✂

I have enclosed the required number of proofs of purchase from any specially marked "Gifts From The Heart" Harlequin romance book, plus cash register receipts and a check or money order payable to Harlequin Gifts From The Heart Offer, to cover postage and handling.

002

CHECK ONE	ITEM	# OF PROOFS OF PURCHASE	POSTAGE & HANDLING FEE
	01 Brass Picture Frame	2	$ 1.00
	02 Heart-Shaped Candle Holders with Candles	3	$ 1.00
	03 Heart-Shaped Keepsake Box	4	$ 1.00
	04 Gold-Plated Heart Pendant	5	$ 1.00
	05 Collectors' Doll Limited quantities available	12	$ 2.75

NAME _____

STREET ADDRESS _____ APT. # _____

CITY _____ STATE _____ ZIP _____

Mail this certificate, designated number of proofs of purchase (inside back page) and check or money order for postage and handling to:

Gifts From The Heart, P.O. Box 4814
Reidsville, N. Carolina 27322-4814

NOTE THIS IMPORTANT OFFER'S TERMS

Requests must be postmarked by May 31, 1988. Only proofs of purchase from specially marked "Gifts From The Heart" Harlequin books will be accepted. This certificate plus cash register receipts and a check or money order to cover postage and handling must accompany your request and may not be reproduced in any manner. Offer void where prohibited, taxed or restricted by law. LIMIT ONE REQUEST PER NAME, FAMILY, GROUP, ORGANIZATION OR ADDRESS. Please allow up to 8 weeks after receipt of order for shipment. Offer only good in the U.S.A. Hurry—Limited quantities of collectors' doll available. Collectors' dolls will be mailed to first 15,000 qualifying submitters. All other submitters will receive 12 free previously unpublished Harlequin books and a postage & handling refund.

OFFER-1RR

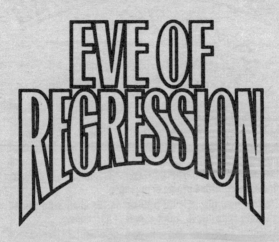

GIFTS FROM THE HEART
from Harlequin®

FREE BY MAIL With proofs of purchase
plus postage and handling

A. Hand-polished solid brass picture frame 1-5/8″ × 1-3/8″ with 2 proofs of purchase.

B. Individually handworked, pair of heart-shaped glass candle holders (2″ diameter), 6″ candles included, with 3 proofs of purchase.

C. Heart-shaped porcelain keepsake box (1″ high) with delicate flower motif with 4 proofs of purchase.

D. Radiant gold-plated heart pendant on 16″ chain with complimentary satin pouch with 5 proofs of purchase.

E. Beautiful collectors' doll with genuine porcelain face, hands and feet, and a charming heart appliqué on dress with 12 proofs of purchase. Limited quantities available. See offer terms.

HERE IS HOW TO GET YOUR FREE GIFTS

Send us the required number of proofs of purchase (below) of specially marked ''Gifts From The Heart'' Harlequin books and cash register receipts with the Offer Certificate (available in the back pages) properly completed, plus a check or money order (do not send cash) payable to Harlequin Gifts From The Heart Offer. We'll RUSH you your specified gift. Hurry—Limited quantities of collectors' doll available. See offer terms.

GIFTS FROM THE HEART

201R

ONE PROOF OF PURCHASE

To collect your free gift by mail you must include the necessary number of proofs of purchase with order certificate.